The

IPO

Conspiracy

R. LaMont W.

Copyright

Dedication

This book is dedicated:

To: Marilyn,

My wife, best friend, and soulmate.

Thank you for your support and letting me write.

To: Phillis Clements,

My Zeta Phi Beta Sorority Sister, my publisher, and dear friend. You were my Sunshine Solutions. I will always remember your smile, your laughter, and your happy face.

May you rest in peace.

I will miss you.

Love hugs!

R. LaMont W.

Acknowledgements

I'd like to acknowledge and thank all of the members of my critics circle. Marilyn Woods for your phenomenal insights, Carolyn Lee for your commentary on my story development, Otis Benning, Tommy Ross, and Carlitta Cole-Kelley for your edits and point of view insights. To George B. Williams, III, M.D., for your medical expertise and Kamaal Thomas for your cyber input.

A special thanks to Genoa Barrow, Senior Staff Writer for the Sacramento Observer Newspaper. Your copy editing and writing taught me a lot about writing. You are phenomenal.

To the Jerry Jenkins Writer's Guild. The Guild is a great place for learning how to write a book. I've gained so much knowledge about writing it would take a book to tell you what I've learned.

To Angela Lofton-Moore for your book design and your wisdom.

Last but not least, Rev. Kevin Kitrell Ross. Thank you for letting me participate in your Dream Series. You jump started my writing career. Ain't no stopping me now!

Thank you all for your support.

Prologue

Wednesday
May 16, 2018
9:45 a.m. (MST)
Gypsum, Colorado

Adam Chandler, his brothers James, and Ralph spent the night at the Gypsum Plaza Suites. For the past twenty years they'd come here to fish.

At the break of dawn, they were on the Eagle River well known for its large rainbow and cutthroat trout. This area is full of deep pools of cold water and a fly fisherman's dream.

Adam waded into the river with his nine-foot fishing rod. He wore a lightweight/breathable wader with felt soled wading boots. The river ran faster than normal due to the large spring snow runoff. As Adam walked out into the river he was careful, gauging every step. He was uncertain how far out he could go. He nearly slipped at the edge of a steep drop. He backed up a few steps, gathered himself as his two brothers waded in behind him.

Ralph yelled, "Are you alright."

"I'm fine," he said.

He found a spot from the drop where the water was above his knees and below his waistline. He cast his line several times before something big hit. He braced himself to reel in his catch when he slipped and fell.

His waders quickly filled with water. He struggled to gain his footing. Before anyone could react he slid into the moving current. His brothers watched in horror as he was swept from sight. They couldn't go after him for fear they too would be pulled into the fast-moving undercurrent.

They scrambled back to shore and called 911.

Friday
May 18, 2018
Manhattan, New York
7:30 p.m. (EST)

Helen and William Grace were laughing and having a great time as they entered the West 51st Street Restaurant. Linda and her husband Bob arrived shortly thereafter. They ordered bottles of Moët Chandon and Voss Sparkling Water. This dinner had been planned for months. Linda's baby was due in a week or two. After kissing and hugging they ordered a large, koshered seafood platter.

Linda surprised everyone with special news. She'd found out today her baby's gender. Her name would be Helen Grace Johnson. Helen was thrilled knowing her first granddaughter would carry her name.

They toasted the pending arrival of the newest member of the family.

Finishing the scrumptious meal Helen felt nauseous.

William asked, "are you okay?"

"Excused me, I need to go to the lady's room," she said.

2

"I think I'm going to vomit."

Her legs wobbled and Linda grabbed her arm as they walked. She never made it falling to the floor, her eyes rolling back in her head.

Linda screamed, "someone call 911!"

She entered Beth Israel Medical Center in a coma. The initial diagnoses: anaphylactic shock. The doctors asked many questions. Is she allergic to anything, peanuts, tree nuts, fish, shellfish, or dairy products?

Everyone knew of her food allergies, but none of those were served with dinner. She was given epinephrine, a dose of corticosteroids and diphenhydramine. They refused to pump her stomach, fearing it would do more harm than good. Blood and urine Samples were taken to get a toxicology report.

Saturday
May 19, 2018
7:30 a.m.
Manhattan, New York

Vanessa Gilbert woke up to noise in her living room. She'd heard her roommate Darcy leave earlier for her morning run so she got up to investigate. She found four NYPD officers were tearing up the place.

"What's going on?" she asked incredulously.

An officer grabbed her arm. Instinctively Vanessa went into combat mode. She ripped her arm away and spun, elbows up. Connecting, she broke his jaw. A side kick sent another man flying across the room. He crashed through the coffee table. Another officer grabbed her. She jabbed him in his right eye and engaged in hand-to-hand combat with the fourth man. They regrouped and swarmed her.

Vanessa fought with everything she had. Everything became a weapon and she threw everything within reach at her attackers. She was in shape and could handle two men, maybe three, but four were just too many. The guy with the punctured eye dived at her from behind, slamming her onto the couch. She struggled but couldn't move under his immense weight. Just as she told herself not to give up, not to give in, she felt the zap of a stun gun rock her slim body.

Vanessa woke later with her hands and feet handcuffed to a bed. Her mind was foggy and she felt as if she were floating. *I've been drugged.*

A man stuck his head in the door.

"She's awake," he said.

She attempted to speak.

"Who are —?"

Before she could finish her sentence, the man stuck a needle in her neck and everything went black.

Chapter 1

5:30 a.m. (PST)
Los Angeles

Nathan Gilbert

Nathan Gilbert's phone rang.

"Who could be calling at this hour?" he wondered out loud.

The job, always the job.

"This better be important," he spit out, reaching for the phone.

An old colleague from the New York Police Department was on the other end.

No pleasantries. The man got straight to the point. "There's been a break-in at your sister's apartment." An early morning robbery, apparently. Your sister is missing."

Nathan didn't need to hear more. He dressed in a flash and left the house. He'd call his wife Mildred later.

From the car, he dialed his superior, Randel Cunningham to explain the situation. Cunningham was Assistant Director in Charge, Los Angeles Federal Bureau of Investigation.

"I'm stopping by the office to pick up a few things before I head to New York," Nathan said.

"I got a call from New York too. I'll meet you there," Randel said.

When Nathan arrived, the office was buzzing.

He wondered, what is going on at 6:00 a.m. on a Saturday morning?

Agents were huddled around Randel's desk when he entered. They were all sorry to hear about his sister.

Things got worse as Randel laid out the details as he knew them.

"We're joining forces with the New York office," he said. A local robbery is not a federal offense, but kidnapping is. That gets us involved."

"I need you to stand down, he told Nathan. This case is too close to you. I don't want your emotions interfering with an open investigation."

Nathan didn't give a damn about protocol; this was his sister and someone had taken her. Without a word, he took off his badge and unholstered his gun. He laid them on Randel's desk and turned to leave.

"Hold on a minute," said Randel. "I don't want you blowing your career doing something you will regret later."

"To hell with that! I'm not waiting on the bureaucracy to do what I have to do."

Randel smiled in agreement. "I knew you'd say that. That's why I called everyone in before you called me."

The elder man walked around his desk, picking up Nathan's gun and badge.

"I've assigned Agent Samantha Jackson to go with you," Randle said.

Nathan immediately objected. He didn't need a babysitter.

Randel put up his hands, shutting down any further objection.

"I know you like working alone, but I'm sending Jackson with you as backup. Besides, she's our best computer specialist and extremely good at analyzing crimes scenes."

"You may need these," he said, handing Nathan back his badge and weapon.

"There's a plane waiting at LaGuardia. Samantha is already on her way. She's been briefed. New York will provide full cooperation."

"Now, get the hell out of here and go find your sister," Randel said.

As Nathan exited, he heard his superior add, "don't forget, she's part of our family too."

Nathan grabbed his briefcase from his desk and snatched a few things he would likely need. As he made his way to the elevator, he fielded encouragement and support from other members of the team.

His phone rang. It was his wife.

"Your parents just called," she jumped right in, before he could say a word.

"They got a call from New York. We're all worried. What are you going to do?"

There was only one thing he could do.

"I'm going to find her."

"I know you will honey. I love you."

"I love you too."

Chapter 2

Samantha Jackson

Special Agent Samantha Jackson was sitting at the window seat of the private jet when Nathan arrived. He was familiar with her storied career.

She graduated at the top of her class at Penn State. She'd earned a Bachelor of Science degree in criminal justice with a minor in computer science. The bureau recruited her on the spot.

She resembled his sister. Five feet ten, played varsity basketball from Jr. High through college. She earned a reputation as being the best at anything she did. An enigma to her fellow officers, she possessed an uncanny ability of piecing together puzzles of a crime scene. She had broken many cases that seemed unsolvable including several high-profile kidnappings and breaking up a large prostitution network in Florida. Her history at the agency was nothing short of legendary.

When Nathan boarded Samantha was focused on her laptop and barely acknowledged his presence. She only looked up when he cleared his throat.

"Good morning," she said with a perfunctory nod and turned back to her laptop.

As the plane taxied to the tarmac Samantha sighed deeply, sat back in her seat, and turned to him.

"Agent Gilbert, I'm Special Agent Samantha Jackson."

Nathan took a seat next to her.

"I'm studying something you need to look at turning her laptop in his direction."

"We're looking at various cameras throughout Vanessa's apartment building. Something's not right. I was told this was a robbery and a kidnapping."

Nathan leaned in, waiting for the "but".

"The first thing I did was hack into their security system," Samantha continued.

I've been looking at it since I got the call from Randel."

Her screen showed various cameras throughout his sister's building. It was a newly constructed building and cameras were everywhere from the parking garage to the garden deck on the roof. Cameras ran the perimeter of the building and more monitored every elevator, hallway, swimming pool and storage areas.

"What do you see?" Samantha prompted.

"I see a hell of a lot of cameras," Nathan answered, his brows bunch.

"How far back does the video footage go?" he asked.

"From what I gathered, the apartment manager keeps the videos a week, before they're uploaded to a server on the second floor and stored for six months," Samantha said.

This building is barely six months old. Everything we want is right here." She continued, tapping the keyboard with manicured nails.

When a camera focused on the garage level came into to view, Samantha asked him again, "what do you see?"

"I see a NYPD Police vehicle," Nathan said touching the screen.

"Is that all?"

Nathan was missing something but didn't know what.

"Tell me what we're looking at," he prompted.

She smiled.

"This looks like a police car but it isn't," she said.

NYPD cars are white with two blue stripes along each side. This car is not white. It's pearl and the stripes aren't big enough.

She zoomed in and pointed a finger at the screen.

"Look", she said. "The size of the font is wrong. And the lettering should be Rockwell Extra Bold. Most people wouldn't notice, but the lettering here is Garamond. The license plates have flash-reflecting plastic covers over them. That's illegal in New York. These are normally used to thwart toll and traffic cameras. In this case it's being used to cover up the license plate of the car."

"In the early morning hours an unobservant person wouldn't notice the distinction between this car and a real NYPD car, she continued.

I'm going to see if I can download the faces from the videos. I'll compare them to NYPD personnel. It may take a while but if I can get the actual video, our lab should be able to construct some photos of the people who entered the apartment building."

Nathan sat back in his seat thinking; I'm glad Randy assigned her to me.

8:15 a.m. (PST)
Sacramento, California

Raymond St. John's phone buzzed.

"Three down, two to go," said a familiar voice on the other end.

"Wonderful," Raymond said.

"This next one should be easy," the caller said. "Our people are in place."

"Good, I'm headed over there now," Raymond shared glancing at the expensive watch on his wrist.

"What about the runner?" Raymond asked.

"She's in the wind but we're tracking her movements. She won't get far. Once we capture her we'll be long gone," said the voice

Chapter 3

Jessica Bane

Jessica Bane entered the Captain's Table restaurant to meet Ambrosia Alexander, Senior Vice President, Cosmopolitan Modeling Agency. Thanks to CMA, Jessica had appeared on the covers of several law reviews, but this would be their first-time meeting.

As she approached the outdoor dining area, she saw him. He was holding hands with a tall, dark-skinned woman with short curly blond hair. The two wore identical bicycle kits. Jessica immediately turned around and left unnoticed.

9:05 a.m.

Ambrosia Alexander

Having been on the road for more than a month securing investors for my company's upcoming Initial Public Offering, this was the first leisurely meal I'd had in a while.

I took the last bite without feeling one ounce of guilt for cleaning my breakfast plate. The Crab Cake Benedict had been well worth the price and the calories.

I'd gotten $30 million in commitments for my IPO and felt I could relax for a moment. Eating outside was a pleasant experience.

I'd been waiting for more than thirty minutes to meet with a client who was either very late or was going to be a no show.

I made a mental note of how bright the sun was shining and how crystal clear the blue sky was. I was happy and excited to get back to New York where I could celebrate my successful marketing effort. Sitting there I couldn't help but enjoy the magnificent view of the Sacramento River.

The harried-looking waiter returned to my table like a dark cloud threatening my good mood.

"This credit card has also been declined too," he said.

This was the second card I'd handed over. The first could have been a mistake of technology, but now I was annoyed, if not a bit embarrassed, as other diners were now staring.

"What do you mean? That's impossible," I said.

The waiter stood, waiting impatiently. I got a queasy feeling in my gut. Something was wrong, very wrong.

I tried to remain calm, but my mind was racing. What is going on?

I fiddled through my purse and fished out $40. I forked over the cash to the server who wasn't all that sly about inspecting it. As he left to get my change, I picked up my cell phone to dial my roommate and Chief Financial Officer, Darcy Higgins. She would have answers.

My phone lit up but gave me nothing. How odd. It had been on the charger all night and should be fully powered up this morning.

As I stared at the useless phone, a tall, handsome man in a dark blue suit appeared at my table. He stood momentarily looking down at me. Without invitation, the man pulled out a chair, sat and slid close to me, in one seemingly fluid motion.

"Good morning Ambrosia."

"Excuse me, do I know you?"

The man smiled. "No, but I know you. You're having financial problems. I can solve them for you."

The man's hand touched my knee with an embrace way too familiar for a stranger. The *audacity*. I jumped from my seat, sending the chair flying from the quick movement. I slapped his face with a stinging open-hand.

"Who in the hell do you think you are?" I asked.

The man simply rubbed his face and smiled.

She's more beautiful than her photos.

Five foot nine, an hourglass figure, maybe 120 pounds. An oval, perfectly symmetrical face, piercing diamond blue eyes and stylishly graying straw-colored hair. It was hard not to stare at her.

She'd be worth at least $200,000, maybe $300,000.

The man repeated himself.

"I'm here to solve your financial problems."

"What the hell are you talking about?" I shouted.

By now, we'd drawn everyone's attention. People at the other tables turned around for a better view of the unfolding drama.

"You need me," he said, looking me over. It was if he were undressing me with his intense gaze.

"If you want to get home, you're going to need my assistance."

I'd been rendered speechless and he didn't wait for me to find words.

"I'll wait for you outside the lobby," he said, walking away with a confident swagger.

Who the hell is this guy and how does he know my name?

The couple sitting at the table directly across from me had heard everything. The woman offered me the use of her phone. Before I could respond, she was already holding it out to me. I hesitated at first, but then took it.

"There's something familiar about that guy," the woman said. "I can't put my finger on it, but he's bad news."

I called Darcy. She answered on the second ring, her voice trembling, bordering on hysterical.

"What's wrong?" I asked.

"Our apartment has been broken into. The living room's a wreck and Vanessa's gone," Darcy said.

"The police are here," she continued in an octave higher than her usual voice. "Our apartment has been declared a crime scene. I gave them a statement."

Darcy said she'd tried calling me earlier but got a message saying my number was no longer in service.

"Where are you calling me from now?" she asked.

I described my day so far.

"I only have a few hundred dollars in cash," I explained. "I'm not sure how far that'll get me. I'm not sure what to do."

"I don't know either," Darcy answered.

"I think somebody is after us. You need to find a safe place. Try to call me back later," she said, before hanging up.

Find a safe place? Call me back later?

I looked at the phone in disbelief. What had happened to my morning? What had started out as a beautiful day had quickly become a nightmare.

The woman snapped her finger, bringing me out of my revery.

""Reginald Pearson. That's his name. He was busted for sex trafficking in Florida years ago. He looks different for some reason, but that's him, I'm sure of it."

18

I sat down feeling like I was in quicksa
I had to look like a deer caught in headlights. I
feeling like it. The woman's male companion s
their table and told her to stay with me while I
make a call. He dropped some bills on the table
away.

Away from listening ears, he hit the one button that
instantly connected him to the Invisible Securities.

"Houston, I have a problem."

"Eyes are on you," a voice replied.

"What do you need?"

Malcom gave what little information he had.

"Give us a few minutes. We'll call you back. Whatever
it is we'll handle it."

When he returned to the outdoor dining area, the
woman had introduced themselves and were chatting like
two old friends catching up on things.

Ambrosia was telling Emily everything about her trip
and why it was important to get back to New York.

"Help is on the way," Malcom Xavier said as he was
introduced.

"This is truly a small, small world," Emily said,
expressing surprise at learning that my granddaughter
Alexandria attended the Institute for Investment Education
that he founded in Moraga.

Emily and I continued making small talk. She told me the story of how she'd met Malcom. I talked about my divorce after the birth of my daughter Elizabeth, who now works as an IT associate for KTLA in Los Angeles.

I was explaining how my granddaughter Alexandria transferred to the Institute after living with my parents and what I was doing in Sacramento when Malcom's phone rang.

He was instructed to go to Ambrosia's hotel room and gather her things.

"A lot is going on," the voice on the other end said.

"I can't talk specifics. We're putting the pieces together. A Black Lincoln town car will be at the staff service door in 10 minutes."

"What about my truck?"

"Get rid of it. We'll take the ladies to the safe house. We'll bring you up to speed when you get there."

"What about blue suit guy?"

"He isn't alone, but we'll deal with them. Just get her checked out as soon as possible."

"We've gotta move," Malcom said, placing a hand on the backs of both women.

"We'll talk as we walk," he said as his wife and I both looked uncertain about the quick turn of events.

"What's going on?" I asked.

20

"Pearson, or whoever he is. He isn't alone. He's got other people with him."

Oh my God. I looked around, wondering who was lurking, hiding in plain sight.

"I not sure what's going on, but I'm told to get you checked out of here ASAP," Malcom said.

What in the hell is happening? This was all so unbelievable to me. We cut a path through the outdoor dining area, through the main restaurant and arrived at the lobby of the adjacent hotel.

The clerk at the front desk started to inform me that my card was declined when Emily cut him off.

"Run this," she said handing him her VISA card. The clerk closed out my bill for a total of $1,243.75.

I thanked my new friends.

"No problem," Emily said. "Glad we could help."

We turned to leave and the clerk mentioned that a package had been left for me.

"What package?" I asked. I wasn't expecting any package."

He shrugged his shoulders. "All I have is this note. The package arrived a few minutes ago. I'll find it and have the bellhop bring it right up."

"No," Emily said. "Bring the package here. We'll take it when we leave."

We rode the elevator in silence. It only took a matter of seconds to get to my floor. My luggage sat outside my room door next to a large cleaning cart. There was a sign hung up that read, "Room Cleaning in Progress."

"That's strange, I wasn't finished packing yet, when I left for the restaurant, my suitcase was open on my bed. How'd these get out here?

"Let me look inside," Malcom said, stepping past the two women.

"Take the staff service elevator, he instructed. There'll be a Lincoln Town car waiting for you at the service entry door. I'll be right behind you."

"Wait," I said. There's a car waiting? To take me where exactly?

I paused. "What are we doing?"

"Where are you taking me?"

Emily raised her hand, cutting off my objections and any further discussion.

" We'd better do what he says."

Malcom peaked into the room and saw five men inside. Two men were in handcuffs, with black bags over their heads. Another man sat tied to a chair. Several guns laid on the bed.

Two men dressed in hotel attire stood over them. One had a gun with a suppressor attached. The other man had some kind of electrical device. He was asking questions when he looked up. Malcom gave him a nod. He returned the nod. Malcom quietly closed the door.

Raymond St. John was standing out front. He saw Emily and I emerged from a side exit. He turned to follow them. Before he could see where they were headed, he nearly ran over a valet coming from the opposite direction.

"Excuse me sir, I didn't see you," said the valet.

"Can I help you?"

"No, just getting my bearings on where I parked my car."

He quickly walked to a black Mercedes Benz. The valet followed him to the edge of the building and stood out of sight videotaping him.

St. John's phone rang. There was no greeting.

"Is it done?" said the voice.

"No, she had some unexpected help."

His answer was met with a cursed.

"You said this would be easy."

"It's a minor inconvenience, St. John assured. "You of all people know I've made thousands of deliveries. This acquisition will be made."

"Remember, this is a low-key operation. Too much publicity could jeopardize everything!" said the voice.

St. John laughed at that.

"Too much publicity! I thought that was what you wanted. Now, you're worried about it?"

"You realize you've stepped way outside of your league on this acquisition."

"We never tamper with people like this."

"You of all people know how we work. Runaways, orphans, single women, and men who have few if any contacts. We don't want relatives or friends entering our sphere. We certainly don't want people looking for missing persons."

"Now, you're questioning my integrity?"

St. John hung up and called the men.

"What happened up there?" St. John asked.

All he heard was heavy breathing.

He clicked off and made another call.

"We've got a problem. The girl got some help and escaped before we could grab her. I don't know what happened to your people. "

"Who helped her?"

"I don't have a clue," St John answered tersely.

"I saw her get into a car with another person. They got away before I could get the license plate number."

"Did she call anyone?"

"Yeah, some stranger decided to be helpful and lent her a phone. She called her roommate, Darcy."

"Good, we've got her phone on our screen. We'll find out who owns the lent phone. It'll tell us where they are. I'll take it from here," the man said.

St. John drove off with Malcom on his tail.

Malcom's phone rang. It was a call from Invisible Securities.

"Don't follow him or he'll know he's being tailed. We placed a tracker on him. We'll follow him and listen to any calls he makes," said the voice.

"Meet the women at the safe house."

Chapter 4

The Safe House

My heart raced as I sat low squirming in my seat. My head hung near my knees. The driver sped in silence. I kept asking myself, what is happening to me? No one talked. I wanted to say something but lost my voice.

We were dropped off at a beige house with chocolate trim in a lookalike tract style neighborhood. The furnishings were sparse. The housed appeared staged ready for sale. The driver left immediately. Malcom arrived 20 minutes later.

He found me pacing the floor.

"Did you find out anything?"

"What was in the package?"

"Who was that strange man?"

"I don't understand any of this!"

Malcom appeared calm but I felt his intensity.

"From what I can tell you, there was no package. If it was it came from Raymond St. John. He's the man in the blue suit. His accomplices were planning to kidnap you.

"What!"

"Kidnap me?"

"Why?"

"I don't know. His friends were short on information."

"All I know is they were former military personnel who'll soon be floating down the Sacramento River."

"I do know Raymond St. John was Reginald Pearson. He disappeared several years ago. I haven't gotten any more details. This whole situation is evolving."

"Information from my security company is flowing in as we speak. A lot of bad things are happening. The break-in at your apartment is just part of the beginning."

"What does that mean?" I asked.

"You may want to sit down."

"Why?"

"The Vice Chairman of your Board of Directors, Adam Chandler was fly fishing in Colorado. News has it he slipped and fell into the river. He was swept downstream. They stopped searching for him last night."

I sat down.

"Adam! No, that can't be. I spoke to him Tuesday afternoon."

"There's more. Last night, another member of your Board, Helen Grace was admitted into Beth Israel Medical Center in New York. She's in a coma. The initial diagnose is anaphylactic shock, but the doctors are baffled by her toxicology report."

"Your roommate, Vanessa Gilbert has also disappeared."

I couldn't believe what I was hearing. Tears fell unchecked and I was clearly shaking. Once again, I wondered what was happing.

"I can't answer that right now," Malcom said. "All I know is these incidents are too much to be coincidental.

Malcom didn't disclose everything he knew. He was always careful and had been warned not to trust anyone, not even Ms. Alexander. She may not be telling you everything. You're involved in something you're not prepared for but be prepared for anything.

"Hold on!" she said. "What's this about a security team? "Who are you people?"

"You already know," Malcom said. "What you don't know is I own several highly profitable businesses that require round-the-clock security for my family and associates."

"I've been talking with my security team since we left the hotel. They are very good at what they do. They are gathering information as we speak. They work behind the scenes and in the shadows. You never see them, but they're always present."

"As long as you are with us you're safe. We haven't put all the pieces of the puzzle together, but they will very soon."

"Right now, all they've told me is that we're going to go back to the basics."

"Meaning what," I asked?

"Money, when in doubt follow the money. Your modeling agency is preparing an Initial Public Offering. You said it yourself. You've raised $30 million in pre-subscriptions for it. That means a large financial transaction is going to take place. That's a lot of money and likely that has something to do with all of this." "It's something my team is looking into. As I said before, these incidents are too much to be coincidental."

I sat on the couch, my trembling hands holding my face as I wept.

Malcom's tone took a serious turn.

"What are you doing here?" he asked. "What's your purpose?"

I was taken back by his sudden change in demeanor, I froze staring at the ceiling.

"I told your wife already. I'm here to promote my company's IPO. I've been getting investors lined up before we go public."

"Why here? Why Sacramento?"

"To be honest, Sacramento was not on my radar. No offense but I prefer the bigger cities with a larger demographic population. You may not be familiar with my company. We are not a household name, but you see us everywhere. Our models are on billboards, magazines, and quite a few television commercials. We're the first company to open doors to the celebrity model. We employ a diverse group of women and men who come in every shape, size, and color. Some say we represent the big and colorful. It was a suggestion from my business partner, Jeremy Richmond. He thought coming to Sacramento might have some hidden treasurers."

"Why is that?" Emily asked.

"Sacramento is the center of the world's fifth largest economy. Two of the largest pension funds on the planet reside within its city limits. Money and power reside in the halls of the State Capitol. The Silicon Valley and Hollywood aren't far away. Beautiful men and women gravitate towards that."

"You didn't answer my question. Why are you really here?" Malcom asked.

"Besides making my presentation to the pension funds, Jeremy met a woman named Jessica Bane. We feature her as the face of our most popular law publications. She's an attorney with the law firm, Ashcroft, Bane, and Carson. In my professional opinion she is one of the most photogenic women in the world. Jeremy wanted me to meet her personally. Have you ever heard of her?"

My question clearly hit a nerve. Emily frowned and Malcom went pale. I perked up at their reaction.

"Do you know her? Jeremy couldn't stop talking about her. He wanted me to see what else Sacramento had to offer."

Malcom finally spoke.

"Yes, I know her."

"I've never met her. After my presentation, I was supposed to meet her for breakfast this morning. She didn't show." "You actually know her?"

"Yes, we have some history," he said.

Emily got up, saying she needed to use the bathroom."

Malcom followed her.

"You okay?" he asked.

Emily, looked at the floor and asked, "Is that the same woman you dated before me?"

"Yes, there's only one Jessica Bane in Sacramento. She gets a lot of attention."

Emily stood, shaking her head.

"That was a long time ago. She means nothing to me," he said.

"Are you sure?" she asked. "Just the mention of her name changed your body language. You looked like you stepped on a nail or something."

"That was years ago. We burned that bridge and parted ways. I haven't spoken to her since we've been together." He put his arms around her hugging her tightly.

"You and the kids are all that matters to me. You know that, right?"

She melted in his arms. They kissed as if it was the first time.

Malcom's phone buzzed and he answered quickly.

"There's been a security breach. You've been compromised. You only have a few minutes to get out of the house," said a woman.

"He was directed to make it to the backyard where someone will be waiting to whisk them away."

Chapter 5

10:10 a.m.

On the Run

Emily and Malcom took off running.

Malcom clicked over to speaker phone and listened to further instructions It was a woman's voice this time.

"Leave Emily's phone in the bathroom by the tub. Turn the shower on hot. Leave everything Ms. Alexander bought with her. except her identification. We'll check her for bugs and tracking devices.

Keep your phone, but do not call us, we'll call you." said a woman.

"Everything will be explained to you."

My attempt to gain more information was thwarted.

"No time for questions. Trouble is coming soon," said Malcom.

We ran out the sliding glass door into the back yard. A brown-haired woman dressed in black stepped through an opening in the fence. She waved us to follow her.

"Hurry! We're running out of time," the women yelled.

"Wait, what's going on? Who are you?" I asked.

"I'll explain but we've got to get you out of this neighborhood now."

I wanted to stop and ask for more information. The nine-millimeter gun hanging from her shoulder changed my mind as she shouted," move your ass."

"The police are on their way. This will get worse if we're still here when they arrive."

We ducked through a vacant house and jumped into a black Cadillac Escalade that was parked in outside.

Malcom asked, "Where are we going?"

"Executive Airport," the driver answered.

Sirens could be heard in the distance. The lady flashed identification. "My name is Helen. I'm with Invisible Securities Corp. We're assigned to watch Mr. and Dr. Xavier. This is my partner EC."

"You guys have a lot of explaining to do," said Malcom.

"We'll fill you in, but first, let's put some distance between us and here," Helen said.

EC nodded in agreement.

"This place is about to get deadly," he said.

Chapter 6

10:20 a.m.

The Shootout

A minute later a brown truck pulled up in front of the safe house. The driver stayed as a lookout. Stone Phillips and three armed men got out.

"Remember your instructions," Stone barked. Try not to damage the product. Eliminate anyone else. Be clean. We have three minutes."

With synchronized comm links they trotted to the front door. One man tried looking through the windows.

"The blinds are closed. Everything looks dark," he said. "You sure this is the right house? It looks empty."

"The GPS tracker says this is the place," Stone assured.

He tried the door. It was unlocked. Immediate red flag. This is too easy, he thought. With extreme caution, they entered the home. They heard running water somewhere in one of the back rooms. Other than that, it was completely silent.

Stone pointed two fingers to the bedrooms and motioned with another to the living room and kitchen. As his men fanned out, he headed through the open glass door out to the backyard.

The man who took the back bedroom went into the bathroom. It was full of steam. He nudged the shower curtain open with the nose of his gun and found it empty.

A cell phone sat on the edge of the tub.

"It's a set up, he yelled. Everybody out."

Suddenly, clicking sounds were heard throughout the house. Doors that were open, closed instantly. The man in the living room found himself trapped behind two sliding pocket doors. Stone was trapped in the backyard.

The driver saw a barrage of police cars coming from every direction. He yelled through his comm link. "We've got company!"

He attempted to drive off, but his exit was blocked. He barreled through a patrol car and crashed into a fire hydrant. Automatic weapon in hand, the man jumped out of the truck and started shooting. He downed one police officer and unleashed a bevy of bullets on the others. He was soon hit by a staccato of gunfire, the sound echoing through the neighborhood.

The smell of chlorine gas filled the house. The men were not prepared for that. It became difficult to breathe. The man in the living room opened the blinds. Outside the police had positioned themselves everywhere. He shot out the window and fell to the floor desperately gasping for air. The police returned a ferocious barrage of gun fire.

After a moment of silence, a voice ripped through the air with the aid of a bullhorn.

"We have you surrounded. Everyone toss out your weapons and come out with your hands up."

The request was met by gunfire.

Hearing the bullhorn and gun shots, Stone ran to the back fence and was ready to hop over it until he saw a partly opened gate.

He tossed his weapon into the bushes and peeled off his shirt. He stuffed his phone and comm link into his pants.

Rubbing dirt all over himself, he ran through the gate. He held his hands up when he encountered the police pouring into the backyard. He looked like a startled gardener. Dirty and unarmed, they let him go.

A SWAT team rode up. Dozens of officers split into groups setting up a kill zone at the front door and around the back. Tear gas canisters were shot into the house as more police arrived.

A block away, Raymond St. John watched the action unfold. He spotted Stone just as he was advised by police to leave the area. He picked him up around the corner.

"What happened?"

"We were set up! They knew we were coming. I got out through a hidden gate in the backyard."

"This is proving to be a lot more difficult than I anticipated," said St. John.

"Yeah, tell me about it!" said Stone.

St. John got on the phone.

"Delivery will be delayed."

The voice on the other end was furious.

"You're being paid a lot of money. Do I need to wonder about you?"

"You know better than that. I'll call you when we're done."

"This was suppose to be an easy acquisition. How'd this go sideways so quick?" St. John asked out loud.

"They had help. More than we expected," Stone said.

"Who? Who could give her that kind of help?" asked St. John.

"I don't know. I've talked with my guys at the base. They've identified some other players. As long as they stay together, we'll find them," said Stone.

"That's what I'm afraid of," said St. John.

"Afraid of what?"

"That they'll split up.

Chapter 7

10:35 a.m.

Napa, California

Flight Time

We boarded a nine-seater Learjet and within minutes we
were airborne out of Sacramento. I tried to process the past
two hours. Everything happened so fast it got the best of me.
The more I thought, the more I was lost.

The flight attendant announced an incoming call for
Mr. Xavier. She put him on the speaker. It was Jonathon
Johnston, Director of Invisible Securities.

"You got out in a nick of time, he said. There's a real
gunfight going on." I don't know what Ms. Alexander has
done to deserve this much attention, but she definitely has
bad people after her."

"You're on a speaker Jon," Malcom advised. "You just
scared the shit out of her. You wanna tell us what's going
on?"

"Where would you like me to start?"

"Who's after her and why would be good."

"Okay, we caught a break. We got a palm print when
he pushed through a glass door at the hotel. We matched it
up with our facial recognition software. The photos, video
and the palm print confirm the man in the blue suit goes by
the name Raymond St. John. He was formerly known as
Reginald Pearson."

39

"He owned the Elegant Modeling and Talent Academy out of Florida. It was closed down about eight years ago. It was a front for a sex trafficking and prostitution ring. He was arrested for pimping and pandering in Florida and Georgia."

"Authorities prosecuted him under the Racketeer Influenced and Corrupt Organizations (RICO) Act, but he skipped bail, got a lightweight face job, changed his identity, and disappeared. For the past five or six years he's been running an international human trafficking operation."

"I knew it, I knew it," fumed Emily.

"He's also a petty drug dealer who preys on underaged endangered runaways, especially young women."

"Someone wants Ms. Alexander to disappear. Since she didn't, the price on her head has gone as high as a $200,000. We're still investigating who has the contract and why."

"One man got away."

"I don't understand," said Ambrosia.

"According to surveillance videos, five men entered the house. Only four can be accounted for. We're investigating that. It all leads back to Emily's cell phone. That's how they tracked you down."

"A call was made to someone in New York using Emily's phone. The New York telephone was hacked. Emily's phone and GPS coordinates were given to hired mercenaries."

"Okay, one guy got away. What happened to the other four?" asked Malcom.

"The driver is confirmed dead. Three men are trapped in the house. It's only a matter of time before they give up or be killed. The neighborhood is in total lockdown. This may play out all day."

"What about us, Emily asked. Are Malcom and I in danger too? What about our kids?"

"No, your family is safe," said Jon. "You've always had round the clock surveillance which I am cranking up now". "Ms. Alexander is the target. You and Malcom are collateral."

"You were in the right place for the right reason but at the wrong time. Right now, there's no interest in you. Should that status change we'll change our priorities."

"It's good the children are with your parents. I'm sorting through what to do next. The obvious thing was to get Ambrosia out of Sacramento."

"We need to buy ourselves some time. We have a lot going on."

"In that case we should go to my place in Napa," Malcom said.

"I'm way ahead of you buddy, that's exactly where you're going. I'll be in touch," and disconnected.

Chapter 8

Napa

I endured an excruciating eight-minute flight to the Napa County Airport. I trembled with fear as Helen scanned me for bugs and tracking devices. Overwhelmed with stress, I melted down and sobbed uncontrollably.

"Who is doing this to me?" Am I going to die? What am I supposed to do?"

Emily tried her best to console me, but none of it got through to me.

"Everything in my life is tied up in the company." Now, I've got this and that stupid IPO."

"Let's settle down, said Malcom. It's been one hell of a morning. Emily and I just finished a 65-mile bicycle ride from the restaurant up to Folsom Lake and back. We need to rest and recover."

"We have food, clothes, and necessities at the vineyard," said Malcom.

"With all that's been going on we gonna have to operate on a cash basis. I have about $500.00."

"There's a premium shopping center nearby," Malcom recalled. "We can get anything we need for Ambrosia."

"I had $300. I left it and everything else in that house. I have nothing, no money, no clothes. I barely have identification," Ambrosia's words coming out as a long whine. "What am I supposed to do?"

"Don't worry about your expenses. We're in this together now. My pockets are deep enough. Consider it a gift," said Malcom.

Ambrosia wanted to contact Darcy again to find out what was going on in New York and voiced her desire to make the call. Everyone froze.

"Is that the person you called from the hotel?" Emily asked.

The implication was clear in that moment.

"Oh my God, no. It couldn't be her!"

My world came crashing in.

"She's the only one I've spoken to today. That's...that's impossible. I trust Darcy. She's my Chief Financial Officer and my roommate. Why would she do something like this?"

Malcom was ready to call Jon, but Helen was already on the phone walking to the back of the jet. She was back in a matter of seconds.

"I just informed Jon of our Ms. Darcy," she said.
"His response was clear. No contact with anyone. No family, colleagues, friends period. We're going dark for 48 hours."

"If word gets out that Ambrosia's been seen, the same trouble at the safe house will follow us here," said EC.

By the evening news, Vanessa and I were the front page everywhere.

"Ambrosia will need a change of clothes," Helen said. "I'll get some things for her. Is everyone okay with that?"

I had nothing to say.

"What's our next move?" asked Malcom.

"Jon is making *just in case* arrangements. He hasn't revealed them. His only statement was for us to be prepared for anything. The tracker we placed on Mr. St. John is still operational."

"From what we've gathered they're still hunting you," Helen directed at me.

"They won't stop until they find you," she added.

"I just wanna go home."
We'll
"~~You~~'ll get you to New York, but it might be a while," EC said.

Chapter 9

10:55 a.m.
Napa, California

Black Panther Vineyards

Upon arriving to the vineyard, Malcom assured us that the place was unoccupied. The manager was away, exploring the French wine region and the staff off for the weekend.

We'll have the place all to ourselves," he said taking a seat.

We'd were watching the news when reality set in. Vanessa and I were all over the television. I realized I couldn't be seen in public. National headlines covered the shootout in Sacramento. A missing persons alert for both of us begun to show up on billboards across the country.

Who initiated that? How did word get out so soon?

Updates kept flying in from Invisible. Every hour it was something else.

Helen returned from shopping. She bought a small suitcase stuffed with personal items: toiletries, underwear, a dress, jeans, tennis shoes, and socks. She even bought a barbering kit, various hair dyes and makeup.

I was staring out the window overlooking five hundred acres of vineyards when she interrupted my trance.

"We have to change the way you look," she said.

45

"I know, I know."

"You're the beauty expert, where do we start?"

I knew it would have to be dramatic. With a deep sigh I said, "Cut off all my hair."

Helen's eyebrow lifted.

"Well, maybe not all of it, but we've definitely got to color it. This brunette will work. We'll color my eyebrows too and this makeup will darken my complexion, I said taking supplies out of the bag. I'd done theater in high school, playing an ugly duckling. I did my own makeup and everything. I looked in a mirror and didn't even recognize myself. I was confident I could disguise myself enough to make it back to New York undetected.

Emily changed the conversation.

"I'm curious, how'd you get into the modeling business?"

"It's a long story," I said.

"We're not going anywhere for a while. Is that long enough?"

Chapter 10

Saturday
May 19, 2018
2:30 p.m. (EST)

New York

A car was waiting for Nathan and Samantha. It took them directly to Vanessa's apartment. Nathan was chopping at the bit. He was doing everything humanly possible to contain his emotions. He wanted into that apartment.

Security appeared tight but Samantha noted the lackluster attitude of the front desk security. That was until they presented their identification. That got everyone's attention.

A security guard escorted them to the apartment. As they rode up the elevator Samantha peppered the guard with questions about the morning's happenings. She pieced together a timeline and sequence of events. Who came, who went, the times and details of everyone's movement. Nathan stood quietly, listening, and observing.

The yellow NYPD tape had been removed. A sign posted on the door said, Apartment Under Repair, Do Not Enter. Nathan dismissed the guard as they entered the apartment.

Everything they'd been told was wrong. Things were out of order from their entry into the living room throughout the apartment.

Putting on disposable shoe covers and gloves they walked through the crime scene.

Clearly a violent struggle had taken place in the living room. The coffee table was smashed. Broken lamps and vases littered the room. Living room drawers were opened. Magazines and books were tossed about. It just didn't feel right though. Whoever came in wanted it to look as if they were searching for something.

Darcy's bedroom looked as if she left in a hurry. Ambrosia's bedroom was a bit dusty. You could tell no one had been there for a while. Vanessa's bed was missing a sheet, her blankets were strewn on the floor. The rest of her room appeared untouched. Her robe and house shoes were out in the living room, on the floor.

Nathan and Samantha came to the same conclusion. This was no robbery. It was an abduction.

"We'll need forensics in here," Nathan spoke out loud.

Samantha scoured the mess in the living room before declaring she'd found something.

A tiny spray of blood stuck to a wall. In the shadows of the early morning, it could easily be missed. In the sun light of the afternoon, blood clearly showed. Samantha saw blood and hair on a shattered vase. She dropped crime scene markers next to the evidence, careful not to disturb anything. She found her prize under an overturned magazine rack. The crown of a tooth.

"Did Vanessa have any recent dental work done?"

"No, Vanessa's a supermodel. She has a beautiful set of teeth," Nathan said.

"Well, someone got smacked pretty hard. It would take a lot of force to knock a crown out."

She finished her visual inspection and took photos of everything from the front door to the back.

"Forensics is going to have a field day inspecting this place," she said.

They went to the second-floor communication center and confiscated the morning video footage. As they headed to the NY Bureau's office Nathan voiced the million-dollar question.

"Where are Darcy and Ambrosia?"

Chapter 11

Saturday
May 19, 2018
3:40 p.m.
26 Federal Plaza, 23rd Floor

The Federal Bureau of Investigation

Abraham Silverado, Assistant Director in Charge, and other agents gathered in his office in the Jacob K. Javits Federal Office Building in the Civic Center of Manhattan.

    After introductions, Nathan told them what they'd found. Samantha filled in the gaps about the fake NYPD car. She asked for a CSI forensics team to go through the women's apartment.

    She uploaded the photos into the bureau's database and turned over the videos. She gave them what appeared to be the broken crown of a tooth. Hopefully, it could help identify a suspect.

    Abraham filled them in on what they learned before their arrival. From the apartment security, NYPD obtained the emergency phone numbers for Vanessa, Ambrosia and Darcy.

    The Find My Phone feature was initiated for each of them. Vanessa's phone was in her room. Ambrosia's phone was not in service. Darcy's phone was on the move somewhere outside New York City. Her calls went to voice mail.
    The NYPD could not determine a location for any of the three women.

The FBI created a geographical map forming a picture of what was taking place at the Cosmopolitan Modeling Agency:

- An ill-fated drowning of a member of their Board of Directors in Colorado.
- The untimely death of another Board Member in New York.
- Disappearance of the Senior Vice President.
- Abduction of the CMA's top supermodel.

There was no clear motive why all of these events were occurring within such a short period of time.

There was no clear motive as to why all of these events were occurring within such a short period of time. It all led them to one conclusion, however. The CMA was a company marked for death.

Their first course of action was to get wire taps of the CMA. After getting a federal Judge to sign off on wire taps for all CMA's telephones, agents got all the call records for the CMA office for the past six months. Investigations into the background of every individual working there were initiated. Nathan and Samantha planned on visiting the firm Monday morning.

Word leaked out to the media. Calls were forwarded from NYPD to the FBI.

A vehicle fitting the description of the NYPD car was found at the West 30th Street heliport near the Hudson River.

The media put together their own sensationalized stories. Eventually, someone put two and two together and it became big news for the weekend.

Agents spent the rest of the evening combining the geographical sequence of events to a crime map. This crime map included names and faces of the company's management team, staff, and outside contractors.

Abraham pulled Nathan to the side.

"I received a message from the hotel in Sacramento about the missing S.V.P. It has all the markings of Invisible Securities. I'll try to confirm it, but we'll wait before we give them a call."

In the meantime, Raymond St. John's contractor was not happy.

Chapter 12

Born a Supermodel

"I don't remember much," Ambrosia said. "All I know is I was born to be a model."

"When I was about three years old my mother took us to see Santa Claus. A photographer took a photo of me sitting on Santa's lap and published it in the Omaha World-Herald. My parents got calls from television stations, photographers, and newspapers across the country. Everyone wanted a piece of little Amy."

"I'm told I became the darling face of the American baby girl. Mom said I was a photographer's dream. My face was perfectly symmetric with natural blond hair and ocean blue eyes."

She said, "my smile was irresistible. Everyone was attracted to it."

"I posed for a "Toys 4 Tots" campaign when I was four. I was a smashing success, nothing short of sensational. In the 1980's, I became the Gerber Baby of the 1950's and 60's. My face appeared on baby products from milk formulas to baby lotions."

"To this day, I don't remember any of it. All I have are photos and videos."

"Dad got concerned about my notoriety after a few threats at school. My brothers beat up a few guys who were jealous of all the attention I was getting. He transferred all of us to the JP Fashion and Design School. They taught me how to walk and move like a professional

"We all learned Italian.

Dad said, "Italy is the fashion capital. You need to speak the language."

"I do remember winning my first beauty contest. I was five years old. By the time I turned 16, I'd appeared on the cover of all the teen magazines from Teen Vogue, American Teen, Teens World, Seventeen, Tiger Beat and Right On! I entered the professional modeling circuit at 15, right after my brother Edward joined the military."

Overcome with emotion I cried. "I miss my brothers. They taught me to be strong, but they were always there to protect me when things went beyond my control. If they were here now I wouldn't be in this mess. As soon as I get a chance, I'm calling them."

"Give me their contact information. I'll put it through. We'll find them. You can call them in due time," said Helen.

Helen cut my hair short and trimmed the front, where my bangs covered my eyes.

"You know buying a few wigs would be a lot easier," she said.

"Nope, I'm not a wig person. Besides, who wants to lug around a bunch of fake hair."

"Please go on with the rest of your story," Emily prompted.

"I'm fascinated by the world of fashion. It exists in another dimension. The only time I see fashion is in the magazines and books that come into my library."

"I attended the Fashion Institute of Technology in New York. It's the oldest degree program in the United States. I wanted to become more then a model. I wanted to understand the business."

"My father said on more than one occasion, age will destroy beauty."

"You'd better have a business plan with an entry, execution, and exit strategy. Don't forget to have a Plan B, just in case."

"I graduated, head of my class with a B.A. Degree in Fashion Business Management. I minored in International Business. I even took a one-year study abroad program in Italy."

"I became a full-time model at 21. I made over $150,000 my first year. I grossed $1.2 million in my peak years. I did runways, magazine covers and posed for everything from Sports Illustrated to Victoria's Secret. My hands and feet are featured in commercials' and videos. No one knew it was me, but it paid well."

"Modeling became my life and consumed everything around me. I changed my name to Ambrosia at 24. Amy didn't fit my image. I wanted a single name that was sexy, exotic and sizzled like Iman and Cher."

"I grew tired of the business at 34. I enrolled in an Executive Master's Degree Program in Business Administration at Fordham University. I wanted my own company."

"That's where I met Venessa. At 28, she was irresistibly beautiful but didn't want anything to do with the modeling industry. Men wouldn't leave her alone. They were always hitting on her. She saw all the sex and scandals plaguing our industry. It turned her off."

"She's taller than me, has this super athletic body and tans really well. We always joke about her changing skin color. Her grandfather is African American. Her mother is Irish. They share the same red hair and sparkling blue eyes. We call ourselves sisters from another mother."

"I talked her into a photo shoot. She skyrocketed into supermodel status a year later. We protected each other and became best friends."

"Together, we decided to start the company

Chapter 13

6:00 p.m.

Napa Part II

I was in the bathroom talking with Emily as my hair dried. Helen, EC, and Malcom huddled in another room. Their conversation was intense and animated.

"What's going on?" I asked.

EC explained everything he knew.

"The shootout at the safe house is over. The body count is four dead. According to the news reports they have yet to be identified. Several police officers were wounded. The house was virtually destroyed. It's said over 1,200 bullets tore through the house. The police found a weapon and a shirt in the back yard. It's assumed another person was there but escaped, EC said."

"Fortunately, we have sources. We've identified the men. All ex-military. All mercenaries. They work for a group called the Exterminators. It's run by two Ex-Special Forces. We're familiar with them. The guy who got away goes by the name Stone "The Enforcer" Phillips. His partner goes by the code name, The Red Baron. They started smuggling opium out of Afghanistan for military arms, but the Islamic State ran them to Syria where their military training and contacts made the business of human trafficking very profitable."

"They've evolved into a sophisticated high tech military style operation. They're not much different than us except for their purpose. They do anything that pays well, from assassins for hire to the illegal labor transport market to sex trafficking. We've been quietly monitoring their activities. They move with military precision once a target is identified. Ambrosia is very fortunate she ran into Malcom and Emily."

"Emily's cell phone was compromised. It's only a matter of time before they put Emily together with Malcom. No one knows we're here, but they'll track her down sooner or later. Right now, Napa's a good spot. We have our ears to the ground. We'll know if there's any chatter." Helen asserted.

"We'll stay here until tomorrow unless our time expires sooner. I've been advised to stay alert and nimble. If we move it's gonna be fast. Jon is working on several plans. One to keep Ambrosia safe. The other is to flush them out into the open. Jon has not identified the contractor but when we do, we'll neutralize that threat too," said EC.

"What about my family?" I asked.

"Your family's fine. Your mother and father are being watched by a few men who showed up a few days ago. Jon has them under surveillance. He'll set them up and quietly make them disappear," said Helen.

"We have bad news; Mrs. Grace didn't make it. Our source says she was poisoned but we don't know with what or by who. We'll find out in a few days.

"Oh, no I cried. Not Helen."

I walked away talking to myself.

"I really need to find my brothers."

I found a bedroom and fell on the bed sobbing.

"Malcom, you're going to need new phones," EC said.

"Why in the world does someone want to harm her?" asked Emily.

"We're not sure but it has to be about money. She and her roommate are not the norm in sex trafficking. They are too high on the profile list."

"Jon's orders are to be ready for anything. He thinks we're just getting a taste of what's coming," EC said.

Chapter 14

Saturday
May 19, 2018
10:40 p.m. (ETS)

The Escape

Vanessa came out of her drug induced state only to find a man on top of her, penetrating her. She was groggy and helpless as the drugs wore off. Her rapist finished, but took his time putting on his clothes.

He opened the door, telling an unseen person on the other side that it was his turn. The man laughed.

"Damn, that was good. She's soft and firm. She's gonna be worth every penny. She'll make a great sex slave."

"I'm gonna have fun with this one," a larger man said as he entered the dark room..

His eyes gleamed with lust. He was hard and excited. He rubbed his hand across her breasts, admiring her physique.

"You are simply beautiful, he murmured to the seemingly unconscious captive. He pulled out keys to the handcuffs and turned to the guys in the doorway.

"Everyone take a hike," he said. "I heard she's feisty. I may be a while."

"One of the men cautioned his friend. "Remember the rules. Don't scar the merchandise."

"He grinned. Don't forget to save some for me. I'm next."

The drugs wore off enough for her to hear everything. The big guy sat on the side of the bed making intimate conversation. He took his time undressing. His hands continued caressing her body until he was naked.

"I heard you put up a pretty good fight in New York. I like a woman like that."

He removed the leg cuffs then the handcuffs.

Vanessa laid there, moaning "Where am I?" over and over. The man crawled on top of her only to have her knee him in his testicles. Caught by surprise, his head was pushed up with her left hand and his Adam's apple was crushed with a smashing right.

He barely yelped. Holding his head up she hit him again, palm up shattering his nose pushing the bone into his brain. He collapsed on top of her.

She laid there for a moment gathering herself.

The man outside knocked on the door.

"Is everything alright in there?"

She moaned loudly rolling him off of her. She continued making sexual sounds, uncertain of who or how many were outside the door. She bounced up and down on the squeaking springs of the bed while putting on his oversized shirt and pants. His shoes were too big for her feet. In his pants she found a wallet full of money. He had a large bowie knife and a walkie-talkie.

She emptied the wallet stuffing the cash into her back pocket. Pulling the bowie knife from its sleeve she unlocked the door. The man stuck his head in. She stabbed him in his intestines, ripping the knife across his gut. Blood splattered everywhere. She looked outside. No one else was there. She dragged him inside.

She recognized the floating sensation. She was on a boat somewhere. Likely a lower deck. This man also had a walkie-talkie, a blade and a gun stuck in his pants. It was a nine-millimeter, Glock G19X. She pulled him onto the bed with the big guy when she heard music coming from above.

Covering both men, she eased out the door. She threw the walkie-talkie's straps over her shoulder, tucked the gun in her pants and carried the knife as she walked down a corridor. She heard footsteps on the stairs and ducked into an alcove. A man came down with a woman in a red cocktail dress and five-inch stilettos slung over his shoulder. He stopped at a room. A shoe fell. He laid the girl on the bed and turned to retrieve the shoe.

A baseball bat swing had the knife she was wielding at his left temple. She caught him before he hit the floor. She laid him next to the girl leaving the knife in its place. She checked the girl. She was alive but heavily sedated.

The man wore a holstered gun, a knife, a Fannie pack, and a walkie-talkie. She strapped on the gun and Fannie pack. She checked the gun. It was a Sig Sauer P229.

She tried on his shoes. They fit. With a knife in one hand and a gun in the other, she started up the stairs. At the top of the stairs, she found herself on a lower observation deck. She saw lights beyond a shoreline.

Four decks up, the music blasted. No one was on her deck. She peeked over the railing. There were three boats, two torpedo boats and an inflatable raft. The drop was 20 - 25 feet. She had no idea where she was or what day it was. She knew one thing— I need to get off this boat.

Holstering the Glock, she stuck the Sig in her pants and found a red door marked "Emergencies." It had floatation vests and emergency throw bags. She put on a flotation vest and grabbed one of the throw bags.

Vanessa climbed down a laddered rope into the raft and rowed to shore. Three minutes later the boat lit up. She knew whoever it was would come looking for her. She pushed the raft into the ocean and ran to a tree line of bushes just before lights hit the beach. She'd gone a hundred yards up a small hill when she turned to look back. There sat a huge yacht. She counted maybe five or six decks.

She could hear voices trying to ascertain her whereabouts. The engine of a motorboat started as she ran into the woods. Vanessa found a clearing with natural lighting from a half-moon. She rifled through the throw bag and found a flashlight, night vision goggles, waterproof matches, a box of food bars and several pouches of water. There was also a solar blanket, water purification tablets, a small AM/FM/transmitter, a flare gun, a dozen flares, a whistle, and some gloves inside. In the Fannie pack she found four Organic Cliff Bars and four full nine-millimeter clips.

With a gun in one hand, a bag over her other shoulder she used the goggles to walk in the dark. She found a small walking path that led to a large run-down building. She couldn't tell what it was. It had tennis courts, a large swimming pool and spa. She walked around it. A few lights were on inside but no sounds. She followed the path to the top of a hill.

Vanessa saw flashlights on the beach. Water was everywhere. She thought, I must be on an island. Needing to find shelter away from the building and the beach, she used the moonlight to determine her position. She was facing the dark side of the island, East. She traversed the top of the hill and headed West.

On the western slope the ocean shimmered like sparkling glass under the moon light. The night vision goggles became her best friend. She stopped to catch her breath, listened, and gathered herself as the bag she was carrying grew heavy.

She heard water splashing further up the hill. She headed towards the sound. It was a waterfall flowing into a small stream. Through the waterfall she saw the reflection of a dark hole. It was an opening behind the waterfall. She removed her goggles and turned on the flashlight. She entered a deep, empty cave that curved around out of the sight from its entrance.

She went as far back into the cave as she could, dropped the bag, and doubled back to cover her tracks. It would be daylight before anyone would find her. She relieved herself, ate two cliff bars and sipped a little water.

Removing the batteries and the sim chips from the walkie-talkies she settled in for the night.

As Vanessa drifted into sleep she remembered her girl scout experiences and the survival training her grandfather had taught her.

She would need those skills to survive.

Chapter 15

Sunday
May 20, 2018
Daylight

Where am I?

Vanessa woke up disoriented. It was early dawn with sunlight rising on the horizon. She holstered the Sig, took out a knife, and went to explore. As she walked and ate a few Cliff bars, she took in the terrain. Standing at the top of the hill she looked down at a long narrow island.

To the northeast she saw the boat. It was a super-yacht, the Espilcse, according to the fancy script scrolled on its back. The mountainside terrain was rugged and hilly. The white sandy beach below glistened against a turquoise blue ocean, untouched. She traced her run from last night.

In the middle of the island was a beaten down hotel. To the North, she saw a large sign. *Welcome to Dean's Blue Hole, Bahamas.*

I'm in the Bahamas? What the hell! I'm in the Bahamas?

The island was carved into small coves and inlets. She spotted smaller yachts anchored on its western bank.

Viewing many other caves along the mountain side, she heard voices. She spotted six people heading to the beach sign. They all wore wet suits. Two guys carried diving gear. Another carried a red and white cooler. One woman carried camera equipment. Another carried blankets. The last woman toted a large basket.

The yacht began to buzz with movement. The two torpedo boats started. Four more men were coming onshore. No doubt they'd be searching for me. She ran back to the waterfall, stripped, and stood under the warm waterfall for a quick shower.

At that moment her grandfather's lessons surfaced in her brain. She found broken tree branches, large flowering pods, and some wire. She picked up several of the straightest branches and carried everything back to the cave. She went to work turning on one of the walkie talkies. While she carved the branches into sharp points, the guys landed on the beach. They split up and began communicating via their own devices.

A man said, "Go to the hotel. Start your search on the other side of the island and work your way back here."

"Brad and I will walk the beach and search this side where she came on shore."

"Remember, she's armed and extremely dangerous. She's already killed three men. We want her alive and undamaged."

"If we can capture her, great."

"If you can't, kill her. We'll dump her somewhere out in the middle of the Atlantic."

"We have two hours before the boat leaves. It'll take us 10 days to rendezvous with the buyers in Monaco. Catch her or not, we need to be out of here in 90 minutes. We'll meet back here at 0830. Are we clear?"

"Why is this chick so important? We've got 22 girls," someone asked.

"You guys are idiots. Don't you know who she is?"

"Hey! Cut the chatter. She has three walkie-talkies. She may be listening to us right now."

One of the guys didn't completely turn off his walkie-talkie. They were constantly chatting back and forth about their mission. She heard the leader ask his partner Brad, "where the hell do we find these guys? She's worth at least $200,000 maybe $300,000."

"She and her friend will be the last ones sold. They'll both spend the rest of their lives in a dungeon on some remote island in the Caribbeans, the Middle East, or the South China seas. They'll disappear never to be seen again."

Vanessa turned off her walkie-talkie and feverishly worked, cutting open a pod and cleaning out its inside. She carefully took the powder from three of the flares and six bullets, pouring them into the pod. She used the wire to tie the top off. She grabbed another clip, took out the bullets and walked to the top of the hill.

Two men were headed to the spot where the divers had dropped their load. The divers were in the ocean. She found a clearing surrounded by dried grass and used the knife to dig a circle. She built a mound of splintered wood and dried grass to start a fire. Using the sticks to make a triangle she tied them so the pod hung down over the fire.

Chapter 16

Ambushed

Vanessa ran up the hill and hid behind some bushes. She'd wait until the smoke got their attention. The leader and Brad ran towards the smoke. Vanessa readied her Sig.

The two approached the growing fire stopping within a few feet of it.

"The fire's fresh. It just started," Brad asserted.

Before he said another word, two gun shots rang out.

Inhabitants of the island jumped at the erupting sound of gun fire echoing across the island. The other two men were about to go through the diver's site but immediately turned their attention towards the gun fire. They too saw the smoke.

Vanessa had mere minutes to spring her second trap. At the end of the path entering the clearing she tied the spears to a large branch and bent it back, ramming a stake into the ground to hold it. She ran a trip wire from the stake across the path leading to the clearing. She covered the wire with dirt and leaves and scampered back to her spot.

As the men ran towards the fire a man was yelling, "Jack can you hear me, can you hear me?"

Chaos spread across the island. People ran towards the smoke. Vanessa sat, watching, and waiting.

The men ran too fast. The first guy hit the trip wire. Two spears plunged into his chest.

The other guy stopped as his partner fell, spears protruding from his back. As he surveyed the landscape the pod exploded. Bullets flew in every direction.

A bullet hit his right shoulder. Vanessa recognized him. He was the man who'd raped her.

Instinctively, he hit the ground. Vanessa ducked behind a large boulder to avoid getting struck herself. Bullets fired harmlessly into the air. The man laid waiting until the explosions stopped. Holding his shoulder, he stood.

Vanessa's shot knocked him down. He forced himself up and started to run. She shot him in the back. He stumbled and she shot him again. He left a trail of blood running back to his boat. She went to the top of the hill to see him speeding off. With his boat traveling at full speed, he crashed into the side of the yacht and sank.

The fire grew larger. The inhabitants came upon the scene screaming for water to put it out.

Vanessa ran to the cave. The closest water source was the waterfall and the stream below. She ducked into the cave, paranoid but listening to the sounds.

The inhabitants created a bucket brigade throwing water onto the fire. With a slight breeze blowing, they desperately needed to stop the fire from spreading. No one paid attention to the cave.

Once the fire was out, the inhabitants scattered when two police officers showed up. They found three bodies, broken bushes, footprints, and a trail of blood leading to the shoreline. Only one boat remained. One of the officers made a call.

Shortly thereafter, the divers came out of the ocean to find officers Peter Johnson and Fred Smith looking through their gear, the food basket, and the cooler.

"Can we help you?" asked Adam.

Officer Johnson answered with a question of his own.
"What are you doing here?"

"We're photographing the reef and fish in Dean's Blue Hole," said the woman named Rachel

The one named Susan asked what's going on.

"We're investigating a fire," Officer Smith said. "Have you seen anything unusual?"

"We been in 55 feet of water for the last hour. We've seen or heard nothing," Rachel answered.

The Officers checked their identifications and passports. "You're from the United States?" asked Officer Johnson. "How long have you been here?

"We arrived last night," answered Cindy.

"You planning to stay long?" Officer Johnson inquired.

"We're here for a few days. We're leaving Monday night," said Susan.

The two officers huddled for a moment.

"If you see anything odd or out of place you report it to us immediately," warned Officer Johnson.

"Sure, whatever we can do to help officer," Cindy responded.

The officer left his card and went back to the scene. They took photographs and gathered evidence.

"This is odd. These men were armed with walkie-talkies. What were they doing here?" asked Peter.

They followed the trail of blood that ended next to an empty boat.

"There were two boats here. Now there's only one," said Peter.

Fred said, "let's get the guys to take the bodies to the morgue." We'll file a report and put them on the mail boat to Nassau. Let them figure it out."

They left the scene. An hour later Fred came back looking around. He made another call, talked for a few minutes and left.

Vanessa waited a while before she ventured out. Hiding she heard Fred talking on the phone.

"If she's on the island, she's trapped. There are a thousand caves around here to hide in. We don't have the manpower to look for her. With no food or water, she'll have to show up sometime. I'll keep an eye out for her and let you know."

The super yacht pulled anchor and headed out to sea.

The divers sat on the beach snacking and looking at their photographs. The island slowly settled back to normal.

By noon they were back in the water for their final dive. Vanessa overheard them talking about getting the photos on a mail boat.

"The mail boat comes on Tuesday around noon," said Adam.

"We'll be gone so we'd better get everything in the mail before we leave," said Cindy.

Ten minutes later they reentered the water. Vanessa went to their site. In the ice chest she found tuna sandwiches, beef jerky, a few beers, some energy drinks, water, and an assortment of fruits.

Starving, she took several sandwiches, a couple of bananas, an orange, apple, a pack of jerky and a bag of chips. Knowing they would notice the missing items. She decided to take a chance. She wrote a note and left $200.00 in one of their journals.

Help, I've been kidnapped to be sold as a sex slave. Don't trust the police. Please call Nathan Gilbert (310) 996-3343,

Ambrosia Alexander (201) 205-2764 or the U.S. Embassy in Nassau. Sorry I took some food.

Vanessa Gilbert

The divers returned to find money and a note.

Chapter 17

Jeremy Richmond

Jeremy Richmond woke early. He'd barely slept through the night. Yesterday afternoon his phone started ringing and wouldn't stop. Most of the calls were from the media. The more calls he got the worse things went. The media wanted comments from him on the status of the CMA. They were looking for something juicy to report. He wasn't sure what to do.

It started early Saturday morning with a call from Darcy. She was a nervous wreck and very close to losing it. She struggled to explain how her apartment had been vandalized, Vanessa's disappearance and the awful call from Ambrosia.

"I'm getting out of town. My life is in danger. From whom, I don't know. All I know is I've got to go."

He tried to call Ambrosia but got a message saying this is no longer a working number. That was odd. He'd spoken with Ambrosia Friday night. She was happy and upbeat.

According to their conversation, "everything went as planned. I met my bogey," she said.

"The IPO is going to be a $30 million success. I'll tell you all about it when I get home."

Around noon he received a call from Adam Chandler's brother.

The evening news reported that Helen Grace died Saturday afternoon from an unknown cause.

Nothing made sense.

He called his CEO Paul Gregory several times. All of his calls went straight to voice mail. None of the calls were returned.

He placed a call to Monique Harding their Executive Secretary. The calls to Monique also went to voice mail.

He called other Board members claiming to be checking in. That excuse didn't work once the evening news hit. Calls between them flew back and forth. Without much information he put everyone on notice. *Watch your back.*

He tried to call Gabriel Simon. He was out of the country and couldn't be reached.

He caught a break. Jabari Cooper, Roman Yee, and Trina Namibian were in the office gearing up for the 2018 mid—year Fashion Week events calendar. The Men's Paris week was right around the corner, June 20 - 24. The Paris Haute Couture was July 1 - 5, followed by a full slate of Fashion Weeks in September. New York, London, Milan, and Paris were all on the calendar. They were busy and never had time to turn on the television or radio or answering the switch board.

Jeremy explained what was going on to his house guest. She left late Saturday evening. He spent the rest of the evening trying to reach his staff Annika Solaris, Beth Myers, and Monica Rodriquez. They were chaperoning photo shoots with a dozen models in the south China Seas, Cape Town, South Africa, and The Jardine River National Park in Australia.

All of this gave him heartburn. His world seemed to be imploding. Focusing became difficult. Finally, he disconnected his phones after calling Juliette Jones. He needed her to find a Public Relations firm. He could handle a press conference but nothing like this.

He picked at breakfast and turned on his phone. He finally heard a message from Monique. She too received a call from Darcy. After a short discussion he decided to call an emergency meeting. Mandatory attendance by all staff and Board members Monday, 8:00 a.m. He instructed Monique to call everyone. Set up a Zoom Video Conference for anyone not there. She would spend the rest of her day setting everything up.

News reports went viral. CMA became a media frenzy. The media connected the dots faster than anyone expected.

One major entertainment show lead with the story headlined as "Sports Illustrated Swimsuit Model Kidnapped! Vanessa Gilbert Abducted From Her New York Apartment Early Saturday morning. Prominent Members of CMA are Dead or Missing."

Broadcast news teams parked outside his apartment building hoping to catch a glimpse of him. They had questions and wanted answers.

A rumor hit the wire. The FBI was involved.

They had no comment.

Chapter 18

9:30 p.m.
Napa, California

On the Run, Part II

I slept very little during the night. I've never had nightmares. Last night I had plenty. I kept dreaming of different visions of my life. I woke up running through a jungle from people I didn't know. I was dripping wet when I woke. Fear of dying hit me. Everything had gone so well.

I sat up wondering my fate. Was I going to die? Were my days numbered? I spent the day keeping myself busy. I fiddled with combinations of makeup to match my newly black hair.

Breakfast and lunch came and went. Emily did everything she could to keep me distracted. Our conversations went well into the evening. I told her my life story starting with the birth of my daughter Elizabeth, my failed marriage to Derrick Johansson and how Lizzie did not like New York.

"Lizzie was actually the one who suggested she move in with my parents. That's where she grew up. I'd visit her whenever I could squeeze in time from my modeling schedule. She once told me she knew how special I was and didn't mine living with my parents. In fact, she was very supportive of me and my career. She was much happier living with them rather than living in New York. We stayed close and still talk all of the time."

She met and married Gary Middleton. They had baby Alexandria and moved to Los Angeles. They divorced after seven years. My parents happily took her in too. Their home has always been central headquarters for our family especially for birthdays, Thanksgiving, and during the Christmas/New Year holidays."

"I think they became a little possessive of their grandchildren and great-grandchildren. Eventually, Lizzie wanted Alexandria closer to home in California but like Lizzie, Alexandria did not like the big city. She opted to enroll in the boarding school at the Institute for Investment Education when she was 12.

Malcom and the Invisible team communicated every few hours with the office. The news kept getting worse.

No details were given on the status of Vanessa.

Darcy seemed to have vanished.

The FBI was now on the case. Of course they would be, I told everyone. Vanessa's brother Nathan is a Special Agent. He worked out of their Los Angeles office."

That was breaking news. Helen made the call to Jon. He needed to know the FBI was involved.

Jon already knew of the F.B.I's involvement in the investigation. He didn't know about Nathan.

"I have friends in the bureau," he said.

"This could work in our favor. In time I'm gonna pull some strings."

Jon made a call to Ryan Norris.

"Mr. Norris, how's that assignment going?"

"The entertainment business is enough to drive you nuts. The musicians are from another planet and the fans are crazy. We're finishing up our last show. I don't know how they do it but after 13 weeks, I need a vacation."

"You know we're three hours ahead of you. This call can only mean one thing."

"Take a day or two off. I have a special assignment coming your way. Call me in the morning. Just not at 8:00 a.m. your time."

He laughed at the hidden joke.

"You got it boss!"

I was ready to settle in for the night when Helen's phone rang.

"Everybody up! Chatter has identified movement towards this address."

She continued talking to someone as we grabbed our bags and left. We left all of the house lights on.

Helen instructed Malcom to leave his phone behind.

Two minutes later we were out of the driveway.

Less than three minutes after we'd left a military truck pulled into the back of the house. Twelve people jumped out and set up positions throughout the vineyard.

"Where are we going?" I asked.

"You're going to Omaha International Airport by way of Chicago to New York," said Helen.

I voiced my confusion and was immediately cut off by her.

"Several jets are waiting for us on the tarmac at Napa County Airport. It has three runways. Jon scheduled flights to different cities. One to Los Angeles with a non-reported stop at Buchanan Field Airport in the East Bay Area. One is going to Newark, New Jersey. It will lay-over in Chicago. The other is going to New Orleans."

I'm confused. "What's going on?"

"Three card monte," Malcom said.

"They'll get here and find no one."

"Not exactly," said Helen.

Malcom continued, "With jets leaving to different destinations, they'll be scrambling to find our exact location." They'll be diverting precious resources looking for us in all the wrong places."

"Wow, you figured all that out in what, one minute," said Helen.

"Malcom has an IQ just below Albert Einstein," said Emily.

"Malcom and Jon grew up together. They are best friends."

"Malcom is responsible for putting Invisible in business."

Helen and EC looked at each other, bewildered. They didn't know that.

"We're temporarily shutting down all the local cell phone towers. They'll think we're here. By the time they discover we're not, they'll look for anything leaving Napa. It'll be difficult with no communications," said Helen.

"I need to make one clarification. We're not going anywhere together. Malcom and Emily are going to Moraga. Ambrosia's coming with us."

"I asked, "why are we splitting up?"

EC laughed.

"What's so damn funny?"

"Relax, Amy, we have a surprise waiting for you. Trust me, you're going to be really happy."

I looked at him. A question mark was written all over my face. They had saved me from a terrible alternative. Now they were leaving. I had no choice but to trust the decisions being made for me but said nothing.

Emily and I tearfully hugged and said our goodbyes. Emily and Malcom hopped on a jet to Los Angeles. Helen, EC, and I hopped on a jet to Chicago. A third jet left for New Orleans with a woman on board.

Chapter 19

The Shootout

Two SUV's pulled up outside the vineyard. They parked a hundred yards from the main gate. Eight men quietly approached the house. As the groups split up a helicopter could be heard in the distance.

Two men headed towards the front door. Six spread out to cover the perimeter. The helicopter arrived and found a landing area in a small parking lot in front of the tasting room. A spotlight lit up the grounds.

Suddenly, gun fire erupted in what sounded like firecrackers went off in succession, pop, pop, pop, pop! Four men hit the dirt. Two others crouched down whispering through their comm links looking for the source of the gun fire.

Two more cracks sounded. Pop, pop.

Their bodies dropped.

Two men reached the front door. A barrage of firecracker sounds dropped them.

Automatic weapons turned on the helicopter before it could land. The spotlight was shot out along with someone sitting in an open door. It lifted up to get away but took direct hits. The engine smoked, stalled and spun out of control. It crashed in a ball of fire somewhere beyond the vineyard.

The drivers stayed with their trucks as backup. Hearing the firecracker sounds they knew they had adversaries using sound suppressors on their weapons.

In a moment of silence, they exited their vehicles trying figure out where the gunfire was coming from. Shots were fired at them. They raced back to their vehicles only to find their tires had been shot out.

"Come out with your hands up." A voice rang out.

Shots through the windshields gave them their final warning. Red laser lights beamed on the trucks from all directions.

One man raised his gun drawn. He was shot several times.

"Don't shoot! Don't shoot," the other driver screamed.

He threw his gun to the ground, exited the vehicle with his hands raised. He fell to his knees.

"Keep those hands where we can see them," someone yelled.

The man was struck from behind with the butt of a rifle, handcuffed and had a black bag unceremoniously thrown over his head. All their gear was tossed into the military truck. It disappeared into the night.

The Napa City Police, Napa County Sheriff and the California Highway Patrol arrived five minutes after the truck departed. All they found were dead bodies, two empty trucks and a helicopter burning in the distance.

Raymond St. John and Stone were heading towards Napa expecting a call that never came. They approached the vineyard. The sky was lit with flashing lights.

Stone tried calling his men. His phone would not connect.

The Red Baron was monitoring their activity when he intercepted a communication from the Napa Police Department. It was bad news. He tried Stone's phone. It went to voice mail. They talked an hour later.

Stone pounded the dashboard, cursing. He was looking at a mess. "That's sixteen men in two days!"

They found out later that one of their guys was unaccounted for.

"We're losing men. We've gotta stop the bleeding," said Stone.

"That's the least of our problems," said St. John.

"Meaning what?"

"The people who hired us are part of a billion industry. I've dealt with them many times.

Their connections run deep into the highest echelons of the super-rich and powerful. On the outside they're white collars, but on the inside, they are brutal beyond imagination.

Sixteen men, that's nothing. These are not the kind of people who pay for mistakes."

"Is that a threat?" asked Stone.

"Call it what you want but these people don't make threats. I for one. don't wanna be caught in their crosshairs.

Chapter 20

Sunday
May 20, 2018
11:00 p.m.
San Francisco

Raymond St. John

St. John's phone rang. It was good news. Twenty-two girls left the Caribbeans on a super yacht across the Atlantic.

It was supposed to be twenty-four girls. His prize in California disappeared. The woman in New York escaped. How she got away was a mystery.

His source on the island said, "she's a lot more than he bargained for, but assured him that she was trapped. It would only be a matter of time before they find her and have her under their control again."

Although his hopes were up, for the first time, uncertainty entered his mind.

His immediate concern came from The Enforcer.

St. John knew his emotions were getting the best of him. He was getting out of control and their difference of opinion rendered him useless.

They parted after a heated argument.

Stone didn't appreciate the threat or the loss of his men. St. John tried to reason with him on their priorities.

"It's more important to find the girls. We can deal with the interceptors later," he said.

Stone wasn't listening. He didn't like the situation. Rage consumed him. All he talked about was revenge. St. John dropped him off at Oakland International Airport. He was going to meet Red to figure out their next move.

St. John gave him a parting comment, "remember our priorities!"

Stone got out slamming the door.

"Fuck you," he said.

He and Red would be no use to him going forward. He implemented a secondary plan. He called Angel Martinez, a retired military tracker. He could find one in a million.

"I have a problem."

He explained the details.

"I need you in two places. The first one is in Iowa. The other may be somewhere in New York."

$25,000 later Angel asked one question, "does she have family?"

"Yes, said St. John. They're being watched, but I'm not sure if I can depend on those guys anymore. You'll be the lead. Up until now, I received no communications from them."

"It doesn't matter. Send me their contact information. Sooner or later, someone will break the silence. I'll be in Iowa in the morning. Have your people in New York ready. Not to worry, I'll get her."

"If her family gets the same help she has now, it may prove to be difficult. They've surprised me three times already. I wouldn't underestimate the resources or who we're dealing with," said St. John.

"I'm not interested in them. I just need leverage to get to her."

"It's your call. Stay in touch," said St. John.

St. John drove to the Mark Hopkins Hotel in San Francisco, grabbed a bite to eat, had a few drinks, and made a few calls. All he wanted was a place to sleep and think.

This situation needed to be resolved by Tuesday.

Chapter 21

11:30 p.m.
Skaggs Island Naval Communication Station
Novato and Vallejo, California

The Exterminators

Stone didn't catch a plane. He waited until St. John left and rented a car. He met the Red Baron at the Skaggs Island Naval Communication Station. It was an abandoned secretive, secure and self contained base that had once engaged in communications and intelligence gathering functions for the Navy and other federal intelligence organizations. The 3,310-acre site made it the perfect place for their network.

Their initial conversation focused on their flawed intelligence.

"Who are these damn people?" complained Stone.

"They were prepared, efficient and well-armed."

"Our only source of information came from that hacked telephone number we got off of Darcy's phone," said Red.

"We can use that to find them."

"When we do I'm gonna cut their hearts out," said Stone.

"We're down to a skeleton crew. We have Slim, his two computer geeks and a few soldiers at our disposal. The problem is they've all been dispatched out in Iowa and New York."

"We need more men," said Red.

"I have someone in mind," said Stone.

"Do you remember Rhino?"

"The weapons expert?"

"Yeah."

"Didn't he turn into one of those cage fighting pros?"

"That's the one," said Stone. "He runs a small company that does counter-intelligence work while he freelances as security for high-net-worth individuals."

"Our intel says he runs a low-key military operation. He has personnel he can call upon at a moment's notice."

"Good, I'm gonna sleep on a plan. Let's talk in the morning," said Red.

Chapter 22

Monday
May 21, 2018
12:10 a.m.
An Airport, Iowa

Family Reunion

We landed at a small nondescript airfield next to empty farm fields. As soon as we disembarked the jet took off.

We walked into a dirty, run-down building with low burning lights.

I saw my brothers. Caught by surprise I sprinted into their arms.

"Well, so much for introductions," noted EC.

I was in tears, sobbing uncontrollably. My brothers were professionals, but their love permeated the air.

"You're gonna be alright sis," said Richard Alexander.

Richard gave Helen and EC a look that said, "we've got this."

Introductions were indeed made.

"Richard Alexander."

"Edward Alexander."

"Helen of Troy," she said.

"Eye Candy but everyone calls me EC."

"Helen of Troy and Eye Candy? I take it those aren't your real names, said Richard."

"I changed my name a long time ago," quipped Helen.

"I like being a Trojan Horse."

"I changed my name because of my good looks," quipped a grinning EC.

"Oh my God, I can't believe you found them?"

"Oh, that was really easy," said Helen.

"Your brothers work for us."

"What!"

"Richard is the Director of Invisible's Mid-West Operations. He reports directly to Jon."

"Edward runs our state operations in Nebraska and Iowa."

"When we heard about your situation we told Jon we'd be leaving. I wasn't sure we'd be coming back," said Richard.

"Jon and I talked for a while before he informed me that you were under our company's protection. Mr. Xavier put you on his tab. We were ready to go to war, but Jon stopped us and asked us for three things."

"First, protect your sister."

"Two, identify the contract."

"Three, you don't wanna know."

Richard turned to Helen and EC.

"I have everything setup. We're going dark for a few days. No one knows we're here, not even Jon. He's given me free reins to do whatever is necessary. If anyone breathes the wrong word within 600 miles I'll know it."

"Damn A! You've changed since Thanksgiving," said Richard.

"Yeah, you look a mess," Edward chuckled.

"You remind me of that high school play. I almost didn't recognize you."

They all laughed at the hidden joke.

"Hey, but even in your older age you're still one of the most beautiful women in the world, said Richard.

"My wife still can't believe you're my sister."

"We need to get out of here. That plane is headed to Chicago. I changed the destination mid-flight to this hole-in-the wall landing strip."

"We're going to one of my secret places. It's a short drive from here. We'll go over the details on the way."

"We have food at the house.

Edward jumped into the driver's seat saying, "we won't be stopping."

"If you gotta go to the bathroom, do it now or forever hold your pee," he joked.

Everyone tried to laugh and relax at his humor.

"How's Mom and Dad?"

"They're fine, just getting old and worried sick about you," said Richard.

"Dad is the one we worry about the most," added Edward.

"Yeah, you know how he is," said Richard.

"All those years in investments. He's still a Type A kind of guy. We have him on an exercise and meditation program. At 78 he's strong as an ox and tightly wound."

"We're not sure who we can trust right now. We captured a man at the Napa vineyard. He's ex-military and a tough cookie. Jon has him. If I know Jon, he'll skin him like a pig until he talks. I asked for him, but Jon wanted him first," said Richard.

"He didn't know very much except to confirmed who he works for. They're good. They have eyes in many places. Once they find out who we are Jon is sure they'll be coming for us.

Jon is counting on that."

"He's working on something but wouldn't say what. I'm sure it's not for the faint of heart," said Richard.

"We're still investigating Mr. St. John. He seems to be the connect to the contractor. He's a well-known sex trafficker. We're still looking into why you were his target," said Edward.

"I think I may know the answer."

The car went quiet.

Chapter 23

Monday
May 21, 2018
12:10 a.m.
Somewhere in Iowa

The Initial Public Offering

"It has to have something to do with this IPO," I said.

"Up until the day before yesterday I'd gotten pre-IPO commitments for $30 million."

"I've been doing a lot of thinking about all of this."

"I never really wanted to go public. I was happy with the direction of the company."

"We are game changers in the modeling industry. We were the first to embrace plus size women and people of color. That concept has changed the demographic landscape of the."

"We've hit home runs in the middle and lower-income communities too. Corporate America is all over us. We didn't need to go public. We've been doing quite well as a privately held company."

"Jeremy's the visionary. He pulled together our amazing talents. We went from a no nothing company to being in high demand in less than four years."

"Gabriel is the major influence behind the idea of going public. He's a big money guy. We don't get along and I personally don't like him."

"He's a smooth greedy son-of-a-bitch. He can charm a snake out of its poison."

"He convinced most of the Board that going public would make us all wealthy. Adam, Helen, Vanessa, and I only went along with the program to appease the others. He convinced everyone it was the fastest way to recoup our initial investment."

"The thing that's bugging me is Darcy. How is she involved? "I'm worried about Vanessa too. She's my best friend."

I wiped tears from my swollen eyes.

"We can talk more later. I need to get somewhere to settle down and think."

"A lot of people are involved in this transaction. It's not just them. Darcy, Jeremy, Gabriel, and others have an interest in this IPO."

"If you want names and information?" I've got it. I've memorized all the players and their roles."

"I love my sister," said Edward.

"She's way more than just a pretty face!"

"Yeah, we want everything you've got," said Richard.

"The other thing that's bugging me is who froze all my credit cards and cut off my phone. Only Jeremy and Paul have authority to do that, but they would have to get Board approval first."

"I have no access to any of my money except what was in my purse. I left that in California. I have a stockbroker in New York, but now I'm not sure I can trust him."

Thirty minutes later we turned onto an unnamed gravel road. Richard spent his time on the phone getting updates on everything that was happening.

"I need to talk with Daddy. He knows everyone and everything that goes on in the financial services industry. I'll bet he can clue us in to what's going on," I said.

"We can't do that," said EC.

"Why not?" I asked.

"Your parents' house is being watched. "We don't know by who. All I know Jon is working on that ," said Richard.

They reached a ranch style house near a large warehouse. There was nothing but farmland and cornfields as far as the eye could see. Richard walked us through the house and his special basemen where he kept an arsenal of weapons.

"Damn,! An incredulous EC commented. What are you planning on? World War III?"

"This is mass destruction in overtime."

101

"I spend six years as a Navy Lieutenant (O-3), SEAL Platoon. I hope for the best and plan for the worst," said Richard.

"Let me be clear about one thing. Nobody, I mean nobody messes with my family!"

"Everyone, get some sleep. In the meantime, give Edward the names of everyone involved."

We'll put together a people of interest list. Especially those who'll benefit the most."

"Let's follow the money."

Chapter 24

Monday Morning
Sunrise
Clarence Town, Bahamas

The Mail Boat

Vanessa slept through the early morning. Mentally, she put together a things-to-do list before leaving her cave.

She surveyed the island hoping to find clothing and some food. From the hilltop she saw the town's layout. A one lane road led to the marina. The city center was a quarter mile from it. She saw the Bahamian and U.S. flags from the Post Office. A large sign identified The Clarence Town Administration Building as several small hotels dotted the beach side landscape.

The divers were back at their spot. When they were fifteen minutes in the water Vanessa crept to it.

There was a lot more food and beverages including her note. It had one word written on it—DONE!

She took the piece of paper and loaded up on as much food and drinks as she could carry.

She ventured out later trying to figure out the best way of getting on the mail boat. She walked the perimeter avoiding any inhabitants. The closest lodging to the marina was the Country Cove Inn. She came out again at dusk to find clothing. She found nothing. She'd have to wear what she had. She spent the rest of the evening devising her escape plan.

Chapter 25

Monday
May 21, 2018
10:00 a.m.
Somewhere in Iowa

The Cosmopolitan Modeling Agency

"Let's start from the beginning," said Edward.

"Tell me everything about your company and the people on this list."

"I grew tired of the sex scandals that plague our industry," I said.

"I wanted out of the grind. I planned to start my own modeling company. When Vanessa, Darcy, and I attempted to write a business plan we quickly realized we didn't know crap about starting a business from scratch."

"Darcy introduced us to Jeremy. We knew of his reputation. He'd been on the front lines of the modeling industry for decades. He expressed interest in our plan. He too was tired of the scandals and playing second fiddle at other agencies."

"We saw a void in the industry. The blue-collar market was untapped. We decided to create a different type of agency. Our goal: capture the off-glamour market."

"We needed startup capital. I had enough money to get us started but Dad advised me not to risk my life saving on a venture capital idea."

"Jeremy and I decided to solicit people we'd dealt with in the past. Those are the names on the list."

"Jeremy and I invested $150,000 each. Darcy and Vanessa came up with $50,000 each."

"Our first investors formed our Board of Directors. Adam Chandler, Helen Grace, Mario Giovanni, Juliette Jones, Claudia Monroe, Dorian Lee."

"Darcy bought Gabriel in as our last private placement investor."

"When we had everyone on board we had $750,000."

"That got us started."

"Darcy and Helen set up our accounts payables and receivables. They established the voucher system we use to bill clients and pay our models."

"Jeremy and I both knew Adam Chandler. He was a veteran executive in the industry."

"Helen Grace came from our years dealing with her as an executive with the Bank of New York."

"Mario came as an independent investor but his years working behind the scenes, of putting on modeling shows, was legendary from years in the business."

"Juliette is independent but serves as our legal counsel. She's a professor at Columbia University, School of Law."

"Claudia is independent and our Ph.D. in Organizational Management. She's the glue that keeps us together."

"Dorian is also independent and an industry legend. She established our modeling program."

"Chase Rogers is our investment banker. His firm is our IPO Transfer Agent."

"Jack Puritan is our long-time accountant and tax consultant."

"What about the staff?" asked Edward.

"They're all salaried employees. They're not vested in the IPO. We decided to offer them an Employee Stock Option Plan (ESOP) after we go public."

"You're telling me the CEO is not invested in the IPO?" asked Richard.

"Paul Gregory, no, he's not. He wasn't happy, but he had no skin in the game."

"He's paid handsomely to manage the company. He provides information to the Board and sits on our Executive Committee.

"Anyone else?" asked Edward.

"Monique Harding came in through Darcy. They were undergraduates at NYU. She's our Executive Secretary, our record keeper, and coordinates all of our calendars. She manages the clerical staff too."

"I want their contact information," said Edward.

"Sure, they're all in the office files. I'll get them when we get to New York."

Chapter 26

Monday
May 21, 2018
New York
6:30 a.m.

The Investigation

Jeremy and Monique arrived at 6:30 a.m. Paul arrived shortly thereafter.

"Jeremy asked Paul why he didn't return my calls over the weekend?"

"I've been kind of busy. My mother is dying of cancer. My brother and sisters arrived Saturday night."

"She's in a financial mess," he continued, She let her life insurance lapse years ago. Dad left her a nice investment portfolio, though. It's in a Living Trust. Unfortunately, none of us have seen it and we don't have enough cash to pay for her hospice. We spent the weekend wrestling with how we're going to pay for everything."

"Oh, I'm sorry to hear that," said a sympathetic Jeremy.

Paul replied, "I heard something about us on the news. You wanna fill me in?"

Jeremy explained his weekend.

"I'm calling an emergency meeting for everyone this morning."

"What's on the agenda?" Paul asked.

"I'm not sure. That'll be your job," said Jeremy.

"In addition to the agenda, we've got the media calling," said Jeremy.

"I called Juliette. She's coming in with a PR firm. Hopefully, they can help us sort through the Q & A's."

"What about the IPO?" asked Paul.

"Are these events going to delay its release?"

"I can't answer that, but it will be a major agenda item."

"It's ready for filing. All we need is the blessing from the Securities and Exchange Commission to release the Prospectus. The Board will make any final decisions."

"Ambrosia is supposed to be here. From our conversation Friday she's got $30 million in capital commitments. We're meeting with Chase and Jack Wednesday to finalize everything. Her input is critical."

"I guess I'd better prepare an agenda for our impromptu meeting," said Paul.

"You and Monique do that. I'll deal with a game plan for the media until we have an experienced PR firm on board."

A knock came to their door. Nathan Gilbert and Samantha Jackson entered.

Paul and Monique were surprised. Jeremy was not. He'd anticipated Nathan's arrival, but not the FBI.

Vanessa never talked about what he did for a living. He knew Nathan was ex-military and in law enforcement. Now, he knew exactly who he was. This wasn't a social call.

Introductions were short. Nathan quickly got to the point.

"The FBI is investigating the apartment break in at my sister's apartment and the strange incidents surrounding your associates. We want names, addresses and telephone numbers of everyone in this office. We want to know where everyone has been and what they've been doing this week."

"Has anyone talked to Darcy?" asked Nathan.

"She left their apartment in a hurry."

Jeremy looked at Monique.

"I don't know where she is but she's not in New York City. I spoke with her for a minute Saturday morning. She said she was afraid."

"Afraid of what?" asked Samantha.

"She didn't say. She told me their apartment was trashed, Vanessa was missing, and Ambrosia was having problems in California. She mumbled a lot. She did mention something about Ambrosia having trouble with her phone and her credit cards. She was worried who ever took Vanessa may come back for her."

"I got the same sort of message from her too, said Jeremy.

"She seems to have vanished."

"We want statements from everyone," said Nathan.

"Who's gonna be first?"

Nathan didn't mention the federal warrant to wiretap their office telephones. He'd already gotten warrants for all of their phone records. He kept that to himself.

"I'll be first," said Jeremy. We're having an emergency board and staff meeting in forty-five minutes. Paul and Monique have an agenda to prepare.

"We'll talk until our meeting. After that everyone will be available for you."

"Nope! That's not going to work. You're going to have to postpone your meeting," said Nathan.

"But we have important business to discuss. Surly an hour won't hurt," said Jeremy.

"An hour?" Mr. Richmond, you obviously don't understand the gravity of this situation," said Samantha.

"People are dead, others are missing. The longer we wait the less hope there is of finding them alive!"

"We don't have an hour. If you're not willing to cooperate you'll leave us no choice but to shut your agency down! Do you understand?"

Jeremy held his hands up in surrender.

"Okay, okay, I've been in the office all week. I've been home alone the entire weekend. I never left my apartment. I've spent all of my time on the phone with my Board and staff. You can check my phone records."

He turned to Paul and Monique.

"Change of plans."

I'll work on the agenda. You two talk with them."

Samantha looked at Paul.

"Where?"

Paul, visibly shaken pointed to his office.

"Oh, by the way, Monique can give you everyone's contact information. You can talk to any of the available staff that comes in for today's meeting. Some of our people are on the road. You can get in touch with them whenever you want. You'll get our full cooperation," said Jeremy.

"I'll be in my office. This is Monique's domain. She's all yours. If you need anything, I mean anything, just ask. We're gonna need all the help we can get."

7:45 a.m.

Four other Board members along with the executive staff were interviewed. Three staff members called in via Zoom Teleconference Video. The emergency meeting started well after 2:00 p.m.

No one heard from Gabriel. His absence raised another concern. Was he another victim?

At 5:30 p.m. Nathan received an urgent call!

Chapter 27

Monday
May 21, 2018
4:30 p.m. (CTS)
Location: Iowa

Stocks and Money

Edward bombarded me with a bazillion questions.

"Who are the decision makers?"

"Who benefits from the IPO?"

"How is the stock distribution allocated?"

"Does anyone have a grudge against the company?"

"If we follow the money we may be able to solve all of this quickly."

"The initial investors are the beneficiaries of the stock distribution in the primary issuance. All investors get shares based on their investment of $5.00 per share," I said.

"Each investor gets 20,000 shares of preferred stock at a value of $5.00 per share? asked Richard.

"Yes.

"How many shares will be available at issue?" asked Edward.

"We applied for 100,000,000 shares but we're only releasing 8,000,000 shares of common stock and 4,000,000 shares of preferred stock. The initial investors get half of the preferred stocks. The other half goes to the pre-subscription investors."

"The rest goes into our treasury as common stock. We'll use treasury shares if we need to raise more capital. Our expectations are to get at least $3.75 per share. Our goal is to raise $30 million in common stock and $15 million in preferred stock."

"You just lost two investors. What happens to their shares?" asked Edward.

"I can't answer that. We never discussed what happens if someone dies."

"The answer is going to come from the Board. I'm sure it will be at the top of all our meeting agendas.

EC interrupted our conversation.

"Word is out. Jeremy had an emergency meeting. We should be getting information on any decisions."

"News has it the FBI is investigating the break-in but they're not commenting. I'll bet a trip to New York Nathan is in the middle of it."

"How does the Investment Banking firm fit into this scenario?" asked Edward.

"If you're gonna ask that question you might as well throw in the accounting firm too," added Richard.

"They're under contract. The accounting firm works on a flat fee basis. The investment banking firm is on a performance-based fee. We haven't finalized whether we're going to have a single underwriter or a syndicate. Before I left they were working on it. I was supposed to get an engagement letter and a letter of intent, but I haven't seen anything. It's another reason I'm so eager to get home."

"Looks like we've got more homework to do. I'll give the boss a call," said Richard.

"Something tells me we're going to uncover a lot of secrets. This may get worse before it gets better."

"Secrets. That's one of the problems plaguing our industry," I said.

"Everyone's got a secret or a hidden motive. Like I said before, there's a lot of mischievous scandals plaguing our industry."

"We've gotta find Vanessa and Darcy. We've talked about those secrets," I said.

"Oh yeah, what kind of secrets?" asked EC.

Chapter 28

Tuesday
May 22, 2018
Clarence Town, Bahamas

The Escape, Part II

Vanessa woke before sunrise to a warm beautiful morning. All she could hear were birds chirping and the roar of the ocean splashing against the beach.

She thought to herself, *I'm running out of time. I've gotta get on that boat.*

Navigating through Clarence Town meant traveling a quarter of a mile through bushes and small trails. Getting on the boat without notice presented a challenge. She'd have to wait until the right moment. Her chances of success were between zero and none. It was a chance she had to take if she wanted to live.

Everything in Clarence Town clustered around the marina and its beaches. The marina was the port of entry into the island and was surrounded by the Government Administration Building, the Post Office, several small hotels, a few restaurants, a pub and a two person police station.

She'd need to travel light. She tossed everything into her throw bag. The walkie-talkies, the flashlight, night vision goggles, the solar blanket, the flare gun, and flares. She kept a knife, the whistle, gloves, and a few pouches of water to last her the 165 miles to Nassau.

Surveying her route, she noticed something familiar on the beach. She approached it with caution. It was the cooler and a welcomed surprise. It contained several sandwiches, a couple of cans of ginger ale, an apple, two banana's and a bag of chips.

For a brief moment it made the morning more beautiful. She would love to sit on the beach and watch the sunrise but eating out in the open was a no, no.

She chugged the cooler back to her hideout. She ate and put everything she couldn't take with her into the cooler while plotting a two-phase plan to get on the boat.

11:30 a.m.

Phase 1. She jogged to a remote cave at the far end of the island with the transmitter and turned on its emergency beacon.

The mailboat arrived right on time, docking the boat across the road from the post office.

Phase II. Up the hill from Dean's Blue Hole, she started a small fire. That would get the everyone's attention. She filled a pod with one flare and residual powder from the other flares. The fire would burn through the hanging pod as she ran toward the marina.

After 10 minutes she heard the police siren heading towards the radio beacon. A few moments later the flare exploded.

The villagers panicked at the sound. Their response was immediate. The men docking the boat, tied it to the pier and ran to help. The fiery distraction left the boat unattended. The entire town focused on the growing fire.

The mailboat was 160 feet long with one lower deck containing a kitchen, a small mess hall, barracks for sleeping and a large cargo hold for sorting and storing mail bags from different island locations throughout the Caribbeans.

Vanessa found a map of Nassau, Bahama in a ticket kiosk. She memorized the location and the route she needed to take in getting to the U.S. Embassy. With no passengers waiting she ran on board taking her knife, two water pouches, a sandwich, a banana, a whistle, and gloves. She went into the deepest part of the cargo hold.

The cargo hold was full of mail bags thrown up against a series of large storage lockers. She found a bathroom and a storage locker big enough to fit her body. Pulling the mail bags up against the closed door she hoped no one noticed their placement.

Sitting in the dark she tried to get as comfortable as possible for the long ride to Nassau.

The crew returned exhausted. They immediately went to work moving mail bags in and out. Behind schedule they complained about the boat arriving in Nassau well after two o'clock in the morning. They never noticed the moved mailbags.

When everything was done they retreated to their barracks and fell asleep. Vanessa dosed off and on. The engine noise and splashing water kept waking her up. The only thought in her mind; *how am I going to get off of this boat?*

Chapter 29

Tuesday
May 22, 2018
12 noon (CTS)

Change in Plans

A major disruption started the morning. Helen and EC were being reassigned. By 3:00 p.m. they were gone.

Richad explained everything he knew. Helen and EC were going back to their original assignment in Sacramento to provide security for the Xaiver family.

Jon was doubling security around Emily's library, their house, and the school in Moraga. He also initiated plans to deal with Alexander Sr's residence.

Richard was told to double security around his hideaway. No reason was given.

Edwards information from me went to Jon. It set things in motion. He knew the FBI would wiretap all CMA phones. Invisible hacked into their wiretaps and traced the source of my credit card and telephone problems.

They all came from inside the CMA.

Jon concluded there was a rogue employee inside my agency. He initiated a plan to force them to reveal themselves.

I got rattled at all of the sudden changes. I wanted to know what was going on. No one seemed interested.

Overcome with concern, I complained about my financial situation. I wondered if my personal bank and investment accounts had been compromised?

Richard tried to calm me down. I wasn't having it.

"I've worked all my life for this and look at me. I'm a mess. I have no money. I'm on the run from Lord knows who. I've lived a great life now suddenly it's being reduced to shit."

I stomped out the front door and sat on the stairs unleashing my penned-up fears, talking to myself. I was taught to be strong, but all of these sudden changes got the best of me. I became lost in my own thoughts.

Richard came out and sat with me. He began to tell me things I didn't know.

"Did you know Dad set up an irrevocable trust for us when you were a child?"

I looked at him with eyes swollen from crying.

"What are you talking about?"

"Dad set up a special fund for you. He kept it close to his chest."

"You don't know any of this?"

"What are you saying?", I asked.

"Dad never talked to me about money. After you and Edward left he stayed busy. I was modeling and I thought he was busy getting rich. All I know, he always took care of me."

"Well, you're not as bad off as you think you are," said Richad.

"Dad was worried about you and set up some kind of irrevocable trust just for you."

"A revocable trust for me?"

"You're not listening, he said. It's an irrevocable trust."

His statement got my full attention.

"Tell me more."

"As I understand it, Dad set up The Alexander Family Trust Fund. If he or Mom died, the fund would become The Alexander Irrevocable Family Trust Fund. He did it for two reasons."

"First, he didn't want anyone coming in after they were gone trying to steal our inheritance. He told me horror stories about children being kicked to the curb by a new person who married the widowed mother or father."

"In the Trust he created a limited liability company especially for you. When you were a child you made a lot of money. He never said anything because he didn't want to spoil you any more than you already were. Edward and I are the executors."

I frowned at that statement.

"He laughed a lot when you were in college. All you did was ask for money. You were a money eating machine. You never asked where the money came from. He still gets a kick about your high maintenance."

"He never told anyone. I only saw it in his financial statements when he was convalesced after his heart surgery.

"That was what, seventeen years ago?" I asked.

"Yeah, longer than that. I know it's in the millions. I'm sure it's grown since then. The LLC is buried so deep in the trust, nobody knew of its existence. Only he, Mom, and his trust attorneys know about it. I'm not supposed to know either, but I'm trained to find out people's deepest secrets."

Edward came out and interrupted us. We retrieved your cell phone from the safe house. We turned it back on. You've got a lot of text's and phone calls coming in."

"Who is Trina? She's been calling a lot."

Chapter 30

Wednesday
May 23, 2018
2:00 a.m. (ETS)
Nassau, Bahama

End of the Ride

Vanessa woke to the sound of crashing waves and a slowing engine. She heard voices of three men talking as they prepared the mail bags for departure. They'd be docking soon.

They were speaking in broken English, but she made out easy enough that they were talking about the fire.

"Mon, that was some fire," said one man.

Another man spoke, "the police thin' it was set on purpose."

"Why they thin' that?" Came another man.

"Captain say police answered an emergency beacon from a short-wave radio transmitter on the far end of the island. It was a false alarm."

"That fire was started on purpose?"

"By who?"

"Nobody knows nothin."

"Captain, say a lotta strange things been happening on that island a few days passed," he said.

"What tings?" he asked.

"There was another fire Monday. They found three dead bodies. Remember those bodies we put in the cooler. We're takin' 'em to the city morgue."

"The police thin the fire was a diversion. Maybe a distraction so someone could sneak on this boat." Captain say the cops thin' we may have a stowaway. Keep your eyes peeled."

"Oh, those cops, they crooked as a broken road," said one man.

"Yeah, that island got a lot of illegal stuff going on but nobody sayin' nothin'," he said.

"Well, if we got a stowaway good for them. I don't care. I hope they get away. Soon as we dock I'm taken the mailbags to the post office and going home."

More unfamiliar voices entered the room.

"You see anything unusual?"

"We searched the boat captain. We found no stowaways," another man answered.

"These guys are the only ones who's been in and out of this room.

"It's just us and the mail," said another man.

"If someone on this boat we don't know."

The men began dragging bags up the stairs to the upper deck. They emptied everything from the room, turned the lights out and closed the door.

The upper deck was filled with clatter. People were moving things back and forth for over an hour. She could hear their laughter as they moved carts across the upper deck.

Suddenly, everything went quiet.

She sat in the dark eating her last banana. She waited thirty to forty minutes before she mustered the courage to open the door. The only sound was the ocean splashing against a rocking boat. She made her way to the bathroom, checked her knife, stuck the whistle in her front pocket and put on her gloves.

It's now or never.

Chapter 31

3:10 a.m. (ETS)
Nassau, Bahama

Off The Boat

From the bathroom Vanessa felt her way to the top of the stairs taking one step at a time. She took a deep breath and reached for the door. She pulled out her knife and opened the creaking cargo door.

Panic struck her. She smelled the fresh scent of a cigarette. Her heart pounded as she crouched low looking down the pier.

At the far end of the pier, under a dim streetlamp she spotted a man with a patch over his right eye. He was leaning against a small white car. She could barely see its burning tip. Another person sat in the car. She immediately recognized them from her apartment. Surveying her surroundings, she saw the beach. It was a scant ten yards from her end of the boat.

She found a short rope and quietly tied it to a rail. It hung ten feet into the water. She sat the boots in clear view of the opened cargo door. Climbing over the rail, she positioned herself and threw the knife high into the air while sliding down the rope. She hit the water as the knife clanged down onto the metal deck.

She swam underwater until she hit the beach thirty feet from the mail boat. She ran towards the U.S. Embassy.

The noise caught the men by surprise. They grabbed flashlights and rushed onto the boat. Scrambling around the boat they found the knife. They searched the boat only to find a pair of boots sitting in the opened cargo door.

Shining lights down the stairs they saw nothing but a large empty room. They scampered to the railing shining their flashlights across the open water. They spotted her shadow sprinting up Woodes Roger Walk.

They tripped over each other, scrambling to get to their car. She disappeared turning onto Marlborough Street and up Queen Street towards the white U.S. Embassy building at 42 Queen Street. She could see the U.S. flag blowing in its spotlight.

She removed her gloves and dug into her pocket for the whistle. Nearly out of breath already, she blew it as hard as she could.

She ran past the embassy guard rail just as the car came to a screeching halt in front of it. She fell to her knees gasping for air. She'd crawled and stopped when she saw a startled duty officer standing in front of her. He'd been reading a magazine when he heard the whistle. He'd been briefed that a guest might show up at any time. He wasn't expecting a car. He hit the lights and yelled through his intercom.

"We have visitors."

The men jumped out of the car and came under the rail when a half dozen armed embassy personnel emerged through an opened gate. One of the men drew his gun.

A woman yelled, "hold up."

"Everyone stand down!"

"I'm Ethel Birmingham, Senior Officer of the U.S. Embassy. Lower your weapon and state your business."

"I need that girl."

"Why?"

"She's wanted for questioning in the killing of three men on Long Island."

'He's lying," shouted Vanessa, still on her hands and knees. "He's one of the men who kidnapped me from my apartment in New York."

"I want the girl!" he said.

He aimed his gun at Vanessa.

A gun went off.

Chapter 32

3:17 a.m. (ETS)
Nassau, Bahama

Saved

The powerful blast knocked him into the guard rail. He bounced off it as Samantha shot him again. He hit the rail and fell flat, face down.

She kicked his gun away and rolled over his trembling body. His eyes dilated as he coughed up blood. Suddenly, he went still. Samantha stepped past him walking towards his partner. He immediately raised his hands.

"You know the position," she growled.

Saying nothing, he turned around and placed his hands on the rail and took three steps back.

"You're standing on U.S. Embassy soil. You're under arrest for kidnapping, attempted murder, and sex trafficking," said Samantha.

She read him his Maranda Rights as the embassy staff handcuffed him and dragged him through the gate.

Samantha helped Vanessa off the ground.

"I'm Special Agent Samantha Jackson. I'm with the FBI"

"I work with your brother Nathan. The LA Office got a call from Long Island. We tracked the caller down."

"Her name is Cynthia Hansbrook. She found your note. We weren't sure where you were, so we split up. Nathan went to Clarence Town. I came here."

Ethel quickly realized the two women had never met.

"I hate to be a bureaucrat but what are we going to do with her?"

"She has no ID, no passport, nothing."

"Her brother is FBI. He can vouch for her when he arrives, said Samantha."

The duty officer said, "hold on, wait a second."

He ran to his desk and came back with a magazine. It was a Special Edition of Sports Illustrated. Vanessa posed on the front page as its cover girl dressed in a red, white, and blue bikini. Her red hair blowing in the wind. The story line read: Vanessa Gilbert, Her Untold Story Revealed.

Ethel did a double take and thought for a moment looking back and forth between Vanessa and the magazine. She turned to Samantha and asked, "Do you think it's better if no one knows she's here?"

"Good question," said Samantha." We can use the down time to find out what she knows and who's behind this."

"Right now, we need to get her to the infirmary, Ethel replied. She looks dehydrated and pretty banged up. She needs medical attention. Those clothes look like she's gone through hell."

"We may have a set of clothes and some shoes that might fit her.

"If not, she looks my size. I may have something that'll work," said Samantha.

"While we wait for Nathan I want to know what happened to her."

"I also want to interrogate our prisoner. We need to know what he knows."

"I don't think he's going to be talking anytime soon," said Ethel.

"Did you notice his face?"

"It's swollen and his mouth looks wired shut."

Samantha smiled, looking at his face.

"You may be right. I found the crown of a tooth in New York. It may belong to him. We'll get confirmation from the lab in New York."

"Let's get everybody inside," said Ethel." I'll call Nathan. A helicopter can have him here within ninety minutes."

3:45 a.m.

"Nathan, this is Samantha. We have Vanessa. She's alive and well."

Vanessa spoke up.

132

"Nathan, Thank God you got my message."

"How are you?" he asked.

"Are you okay?

"No, I'm not but I'll recover," Vanessa said. "The summers we spent with Grampa saved me. I remembered everything he taught us. It kept me alive."

"I'm on my way. I'll be there in a couple of hours."

"No, wait! I left some things on the island you might need."

"I hid a red and white cooler in a cave near a rundown hotel not far from the Dean's Blue Hole. There's a waterfall and a small stream. You can't miss it. It's near the top of the hill where I started a fire. Behind the waterfall is the cave. I have walkie-talkies, guns and a lot of other stuff."

"There's a super-yacht called the Espilce heading towards Monaco with twenty-two girls. I was supposed to be number twenty-three. They're going to be auctioned as sex slaves. We've gotta stop them. I can tell you more when you get here.

"Samantha is my partner", he said. "Tell her everything you know. I'll wait until sunlight. If I get lost I'll call you."

"How many men are with you?" Vanessa asked.

"Two plus the pilot, why?"

"Don't trust the local cops. One of them is an informant. I overheard him talking to someone right after the ship left."

Vanessa turned to Samanth as the phone disconnected.

"You said you work with Nathan. I know my brother. He usually works alone."

"Now you're his partner?"

Chapter 33

Wednesday
9:00 a.m. (CST)
Carter Lake, Iowa

The Mistake

Richard Alexander, Sr., and his wife Allison moved into a secluded neighborhood on the shoreline of Carter Lake. Their modest 2,800 square foot, 3-bedroom, 2.5 bath home sat on one third of an acre. They downsized shortly upon Richard's retirement and after their granddaughter, Alexandria moved to California and off to boarding school.

Allison had watched the news. The broadcasts were full of sensationalized stories about her daughter. She was worried sick, hardly able to talk. Richard tried calling Ambrosia several times with no avail. He called his sons Richard Jr, and Edward. Their calls went to voice mail. Frustrated he called them again and again. Finally, he left his oldest son a long message ranting about a lot of things going on inside his sister's modeling company. He reached a conclusion that there was a conspiracy behind her taking her company public.

Early that morning he found an envelope stuck in his front door. The note inside was from Richard Jr. It came with good news and a warning.

It read: *Ambrosia is safe. She's with Edward and I. Bad people may be coming to the house. Don't answer the door or talk to the media.* Stay close to home. Go out only if necessary. I'll call you soon, Jr.

Several reporters and a television station called with inquiries. All were turned down.

Richard Sr. went into the basement to check his weapons. He owned a Remington, 12 gauge shot gun, a Remington Model 700, 30-6 Springfield rifle, several handguns including a Sig Sauger P238 and a Colt Python .357 Magnum revolver.

The note did not tell him people were watching his house, but he noted the appearance of a black van circling the neighborhood day before yesterday.

Today, Richard wanted out of the house. He felt like a caged animal. He figured he'd go fishing on the lake across the walking trail behind his house.

He noticed the gardening crew out front. That was unusual. Their regular day was Thursday's, mid-day. He put on a jacket to cover his .357 magnum shoulder holster. He went out and questioned one of the guys.

"We're rotating crews this week," he said.

"If you have any questions, the supervisor will be here in an hour. You can talk to him about the change."

Angel Martinez and two other men circled the house several times in a black van marked "Flowers to Your Door." He hadn't counted on the presence of the yard crew. He planned to use them as hostages to find Ambrosia. There were too many people around to move on them right now. He'd have to revise his plans.

Martinez called St. John.

"I'm in front of the parents house. The gardeners are here. I wasn't expecting them today. They're scheduled for tomorrow. It may be another hour before they leave. I'll call you when I have them."

Immediately, St. Johns' red flag went up. He started asking questions. He demanded descriptions of the gardening crew and how many of them were there.

"Do you notice any suspicious behavior?," he asked. "Do they have any visible weapons?"

"No, they look like typical yard guys. They're wearing identical company uniforms, mowing the lawn, and trimming the bushes."

Angel laughed, "are you being paranoid?"

"I hope not. Red and Stone have lost more men than I can count in the past five days. Whoever helped her escape is exceptionally good. I don't want any more surprises."

"From what I can see there's about nine of them. A few Mexicans, some Black dudes and a couple of White guys. No bulging weapons from what I can see. This is a nice area in an upscale community. They live on a large piece of property almost a half-acre. Not a lot of activity from what I can tell. Looks like these guys are going to be a while. We'll wait until they're gone."

"Stop stressing. We'll take them sooner or later," said Angel.

They drove off circling back every thirty to forty minutes. The last time they circled the block they saw one person, a woman pushing a baby stroller.

She hardly gave them a glance focusing on the baby in the stroller. There was actually an iPad with a hidden camera inside the carriage. She videotaped their faces including the make and model of their van. When they were out of sight, she made a call.

Chapter 34

Captured

Red was on the phone with Jacob.

"Kyle and I are riding with Angel, abiding time."

"We'll call you when we have them."

"Did you receive the video equipment and other equipment I ordered for you? he asked.

"Yes, we've got everything."

"Good, I want to make an example out of them."

11:05 a.m.
Carter Lake, Iowa

Richard, Sr., was fishing when a man approached. He pulled his gun and waited for him to get close. He spun with the gun aimed at his head.

"Whoa, whoa Mr. Alexander," his hands in the air holding an iPad.

"I have a FaceTime call for you." It's your son Jr."

His son smile through the screen.

"Dad, relax and put the gun away. These guys are with me."

Richard Sr. smiled back.

"He just scared the shit outta me. He's good, I almost didn't hear him."

"Dad, I got your messages. Right now, we have a situation brewing. Some men may be coming to the house. I'm sure their intentions are not good. I'm certain it has something to do with Sis. I need you and Mom to go into the basement. My men will take care of them."

"If you're talking about the guys in the black van, I already know about them. Two guys showed up Sunday. A third guy showed up yesterday. You know I can handle these guys."

Richard Jr. responded, "I know you can, but these guys are military pros. I don't want any gun fire in the neighborhood. I want to capture them quietly. I need you to trust me. Please go into the basement. If anyone comes down you can shoot to kill. I'll call you when it's safe. Okay?"

"Sure, whatever you say son, but if someone opens that door—."

"I got it Dad. Thanks, I'll be in touch."

1:35 p.m.

The gardeners were gone when the van turned the corner. A large forklift sat two doors down the street, its motor running. In front of the Alexander house was a large red container. Its doors were open. It had just been taken off a truck. The van pulled in behind it and parked.

Suddenly, the forklift rammed the back of the van.

Men sprang from the bushes surrounding the house peppering the van with M249 light machine guns, suppressors attached. They peppered the van with bullets disabling the engine in the process. They shot out the windows. The men ducked low in their seats. Two canisters of incapacitating agents flew through the windows. The attack ended in less than a minute.

The forklift picked up the van and shoved it into the container. It was loaded onto the flatbed truck. Forty-five minutes later the truck arrived at a warehouse next to a ranch style farmhouse.

Edward Alexander came out to greet them.

Chapter 35

12:45 p.m.
Somewhere in Iowa

Oh, S__!

The men became conscience. They found themselves strapped to metal chairs facing each other. They were nude in a tub of water. Several armed men walked around them. The bags over their heads were lifted. Edward spoke.

"You boys made a fatal mistake. Tell me everything you know and maybe you can walk out of here alive."

The rags in their mouths were pulled.

"Let's start with Sargent Martinez."

"I got two words. Fuck you," Martinez spat back.

A surge of electricity shot through their bodies. Each man screamed.

"That's a small taste of what's in store for you," said Edward.

"Look around. You're in a soundproof bunker forty miles in the middle of farmland. No one is going to hear you scream, no one is coming to save you."

"Here's another question. Who's the leader?"

No one spoke.

Rags were stuffed back into their mouths.

Once again muffled, another jolt of electricity hit them. This one lasted far longer than the first.

Edward walked around them playing with a red button. He pushed the button turning it on and off.

After a few minutes of silence he said, "this is really going to hurt."

He raised his hand ready to give them a super jolt when Kyle struggled trying to say something. His rag was roughly removed.

"Wait, wait, we've been here since Saturday night. We work for our commanding officer, The Red Baron. We don't know who Martinez works for. He showed up yesterday. We were told to follow his lead."

Jacob grunted loudly. His rag was pulled from his mouth.

"Kyle you talk too damn much. If you're going to kill us do it now and save us your pain in the ass questions."

Edward hit the button, holding it a full five seconds. Electricity charged through their bodies causing Jacob's nose to bleed.

"I wasn't talking to you, asshole."

"The next time you pop off I'm gonna fry your ass one butt at a time. I can do this all day and night. Scream as much as you like."

"All I know is we're supposed to call Red when we have the targets in our possession," said Kyle.

"Then what?"

"I don't know. All he said was we're supposed to make examples of them."

"Okay Sargent, who do you work for and what's your business with my family?"

"I'm not telling you shit."

"Okay, in that case I've got no use for you."

Edward looked back and forth at Jacob and Kyle. He pulled out a nine-millimeter pistol, suppressor attached and pointed it at Angel's head. A popping sound resounded through the room. Angel's head spattered like a honey dew melon all over them.

Richard stood in a corner observing.

"Oh, Edward you spoiled my fun," he said.

"I was going to cut him into little pieces."

"Now, I've only got two to play with."

He pulled out a large bowie knife and sliced Jacob's right leg just below his groin.

"Bleed on that a while," he said.

He walked out of the building.

I met him at the door of the house.

"I need to talk to Dad."

"Not now, I caught some guys scouting their house. I need to interrogate them."

"I need to talk to Dad now. It's important."

Richard thought for a moment. He consulted with Edward.

He remembered his Dad's voice mail.

He went to the basement and came back with a box.

"Okay, we have thirty minutes."

"I hope this is as important as you think it is. But we've gotta be quick," he said.

We drove off.

During the ride he explained.

"Dad's telephone has been compromised. Whoever is behind all of this is connected to these guys. I need to know what they know. We're going to a safe place where your call can't be traced."

We rode in silence.

Ten miles later we stopped at an abandoned shed in the middle of a corn field.

Richard pulled out the box and several cell phones.

"What are those?"

"These are cell phone scramblers. They're designed to stop a hacker from locating the original cell phone. Since Dad's phone is tapped. I need to scramble the tap. When they figure out where this phone is located we'll be gone. If they find this location they won't find us. They'll find a bigger problem."

He called his father putting Ambrosia on the line.

"Daddy!"

"Amy is that you?"

The delight in his voice was heard.

"Yes, it's me."

"Are you okay?"

"Yes, I'm with Jr. and Edward."

Richard gave me the hurry up sign.

"I can't talk long but I need your advice."

"What is it?"

"I've been marketing an Initial Public Offering for my company."

"Yes, I know all about the IPO and the Dog and Pony Show presentations," he said. "How's it going?"

"I got my commitments. I met my bogey."

"You raised $30 million?"

"Yes, I did."

"Congratulations honey. Good for you."

"I believe all of my problems have something to do with the IPO."

"Is there an alternative to it?"

"If I can come up with an alternative solution, I may be able to turn this madness around."

He hesitated for a moment and said, "you have two alternatives."

"One option is to go direct. That means instead of using an underwriter you go directly to foreign subscribers. If they agree, you can get listed directly on the NASDAQ. It will eliminate the middleman. The key is to get foreign subscribers to buy in."

"The second one is called a Blank Check or a Special Purpose Acquisition Company. They're basically one and the same. A Blank Check is for companies with no assets. The SPAC is for companies that raises capital to acquire or merge with another company in a takeover situation. It's rarely used."

"Trying to get pre-subscribers to invest in either of these may not work for you. These are complicated transactions and you're well established. That may turn off your investors."

"I don't recommend either."

"Stick with the IPO."

"I have people who can help you lock everything down."

"By the way, I've been doing my own investigation on your company. A couple of your people are having serious financial problems."

"Really! Who?"

Before he could finish, Richard Jr. interrupted him.

"Dad, we've gotta go."

He disconnected the call.

Before they left, Richard rigged the door to a timer. A bomb would explode five seconds after the door opened.

As we drove back, I express my unhappiness the call ended so quickly.

"Dad said some people in my company are having serious financial problems. You didn't give him time to tell me who they were."

"He left me a similar message but not a lot of details," said Richard.

"We ran out of time. We'll call him back at another time."

I started grumbling.

He raised his big brother voice and repeated himself.

"You're not listening."

"I told you the men we captured are extremely dangerous. Our intel says these guys are mercenaries."

"They had video equipment and a bunch of torture tools with them."

"I can't imagine what they would have done if we hadn't got there in time."

"They would have killed Mom and Dad in a heartbeat without thought or remorse."

"Calling Dad was risky and dangerous."

"I did it just for you. I wanted them to hear your voice."

"That call could have put all of our lives in jeopardy."

"At this stage I can't risk that."

"I need to get back and find out what I can from them."

His tone registered. He got my attention.

I took some deep breaths and sighed. He softly grabbed my hand.

"Don't worry."

"Now that I know someone in your company is having financial problems, it makes our people of interest a smaller circle. It'll be easier to find out who they are.

"When we finish with these guys we're going to New York."

"What are you going to do with those guys?"

He looked over at me and held my hand tighter but said nothing.

He drove staring at the road.

I understood.

Chapter 36

Wednesday
1:00 p.m.
Nassau, Bahamas

Reunited

Nathan arrived at the U.S. Embassy with the red and white cooler. He wanted to see his sister, but Samantha sat him down first and explained her ordeal.

When they met, she wept on his shoulder for a long time.

"You were right about the police," he said.

"They wanted to know what we were up too. I told them to get lost. We found your box of goodies. You've got quite a collection. Tell me everything."

Vanessa started from the beginning. She broke down sobbing when describing how she woke up drugged and chained to a bed with a man on top of her. She described her escape.

"They came looking for me."

"I was listening to a conversation between Brad and someone else before I shot them."

"I recognized the man from the boat. I shot that son-of-a-bitch three times. He crashed a torpedo boat into the yacht. I watched it sink."

"They're rendezvousing with people in Monaco. There's a Monte-Carlo Television Festival. It's a big deal. They're going to use the festival as cover to mask a sex-slave auction. A lot of rich and famous people are going to be there."

"Tell me about the boat?" he asked.

"The boat is a super yacht. I saw the name Espilce on the back of the upper deck. It has two helicopter pads. Listening to the men's conversation, the boat's a rental. I wasn't on it very long. I don't know much more than that."

"The mail guys were chatting a lot about the illegal stuff happing on Long Island, but no one is talking. I think one of the local policemen is on their payroll. It seems to be a transfer point for women sold into a sex trafficking network."

"Most of the women come from Canada, the eastern seaboard, Puerto Rico all the way to Argentina."

"Nathan said, "I have some bad news about your company. Adam Chandler drowned in a fishing expedition. We're looking for him but haven't found him yet."

He told her the rest. Helen Grace had been poisoned, Gabriel Simon, Ambrosia and Dacy were all unaccounted for."

"We're getting outside intel that someone inside your organization has gone rogue.

She heaved deep breaths covering her face with both hands to hide her tears.

"Ambrosia's my best friend, she got me into this business. I'll bet it's about that IPO. It's going to be worth millions. The people you named were opposed to the idea except Gabriel. He kept pushing it. We've talked a lot about him and his secrets."

"Can you stop the auction?"

"Right now, the FBI doesn't have jurisdiction in foreign countries," said Nathan.

"We don't but I know some people. They don't have jurisdictional boundaries. They may be able to help," said Samantha.

Nathan smiled looking at Vanessa.

"I told you she's my partner."

"I'm all ears."

"What you got?"

Chapter 37

Confessions

Edward silently played with an on and off button when Richard entered the warehouse to listen to the interrogation.

"I'm pissed!" said Edward.

"You tried to kidnap my sister. You're responsible for killing some of her people. Now, you're at my parents' home. This is your last chance."

"State your business with my family!"

"Who do you report to?"

"The Red Baron," said Kyle.

"Who is this Red Baron?"

"What's his plan?"

"Red was our team leader while we were on assignment in Afghanistan. In his mind he knew the war wouldn't last forever. We knew how to survive in a war environment. we were trained to hunt, defend and kill. He'd often talk about what would happen when we returned home. Many of us did not have any other skillsets. How were we going to survive in a non-war time climate?"

"We'd end up like many other war time vets. We'd get an honorable discharge upon our separation from active duty. Maybe we'd get a medal and a DD214. That gets you nothing more than a plot in a military cemetery. He didn't want to become homeless, suffer from mental illness or end up living under the freeway begging for money to survive. To avoid any of that, he started looking for other means of income."

"Red met Stone who was trading arms for opium and smuggling them into the U.S. He was making some serious money. But it came with a price. The people he dealt with were turncoats and blood sucking vampires who would turn on him as soon as things got bad."

"They met St. John in dealing with refugees coming out of Syria. The two of them started working with his human trafficking network. A bunch of us went to work for them until we returned home."

"We haven't seen Red or Stone since we left Iraq. We relocated to the east coast. They went west. We work on assignments through telephone calls and text messages out of our New York field house. Our assignments cover the entire Atlantic coast south to the mid-west."

"Working with St. John became easy money. We captured women and children. We turned them over to St John. He used his infrastructure to sell them.

"We hardly got our hands dirty. St. John made us hundreds of thousands of dollars.

"Where's his base of operations? asked Richard.

Jacob finally spoke.

"All we know is their command center is somewhere in Northern California. This was a special assignment to capture the girl's parents and report back when we had them."

"What's the video and torture equipment for?"

Neither made a response.

The rags were stuffed into their mouths. Several long jolts of electricity followed as both men screamed. They began to sweat. Blood poured out of their noses. Breathing became difficult.

Edward moved wires around. He clipped them to some very private body parts.

"Somebody needs to talk to me real soon," he said.

Another charge hit them. Through his rag Kyle could be heard crying.

"When his rag was removed Kyle pleaded for mercy.

Oh God, please stop, please stop. I don't know any more than what I've told you."

"Kyle Benson or should I call you Staff Sargent Kyle Benson? Here's what we're going to do," said Edward.

"You're going to call this Mr. Baron. You'll do exactly as I say, or you will suffer. Do I make myself clear?"

He nodded, yes, he understood.

"Mr. Randel or should I call you Corporal Jacob Randel? You're bleeding out. It doesn't look good for the home team."

Edward had tied a knot above the cut to slow the blood pumping out of the man's leg, but he was still bleeding.

He asked, "are you ready to cooperate?"

Randel looked up at him as Edward was ready to flip the switch. Through his rag you could hear him say, "Wait, wait! The rag was pulled.

"What do you want to know?"

"Everything," said Edward.

"Our first assignment was to capture a red-headed model in New York. We did that putting her on a helicopter to the Bahamas.

When the girl in California got away we split up. We were assigned to Iowa to watch her parents. Our plan was to grab her parents and extract information. If she showed up we were to do her like we did her roommate and ship her to the Caribbeans. After that our orders are to go back to New York to find some girl name Darcy."

Richard asked, "Staff Sargent Benson. How does this network operate and where are the girls going?"

"St. John planned to sell the girls at an auction in Monaco."

"Our job is the same as always. Capture runaway girls, orphans, and single women in bars. We'd quietly make them disappear. They're flown to the Caribbeans. Our jobs are over until we get new assignments."

Richard asked, "Who's the leader of your crew?"

Kyle looked over and nodded at Jacob.

He called Red and put Jacob on speaker phone. Edward stood next to him, a gun rubbing his forehead.

"Is it done?," Red asked.

"Yes, said Jacob. "We have them. But the girl hasn't shown up. What do you want us to do with them?"

"Set up the video and record the interrogation."

"Start with the father. Make the mother watch. Have them call their daughter or someone close to her who can locate her."

"If they don't cooperate you know the drill. One finger at a time, down to the toes. Work your way from the father to the mother. One of them will give us something."

"And then what?"

"Kill them. Make it messy and send the video to Slim. I'll take it from there. You and Kyle wait overnight. If she's not seen by tomorrow, go to New York and wait for further instructions."

"A girl named Darcy is moving around but Slim is tracking her. I want her alive. She'll be a bonus. If not, you know what to do. I don't want her body found."

"Your contact's name is Rhino. He's expecting you. We've got some cleanup work to do here but I need that video."

"What's going on in California?" Jacob asked.

"Follow your orders soldier. Do what you're paid to do and don't ask questions."

"Call me when you're done. Now, let me talk to Kyle."

The call dropped.

Red redialed. It went to voice mail.

Suddenly, he got a strange feeling.

Chapter 38

The Set Up

Richard turned on Angel's phone and redialed the last number. He put Jacob on the line.

St. John answered, "Martinez, how did it go?"

"This is Jacob. It didn't go well. We ran into trouble. But we've got the girl, Ambrosia. What do you want us to do with her?"

"Go to the Eppley Airport near Omaha International. I'll have a private jet meet you. My people will handle the shipping."

What's going on with Red? He seems short tempered."

"They botched the job here. Stone is frustrated and looking to clean up his mess."

"Tell me about the trouble?"

"The girl showed up with company. Things got ugly. Her parents were badly injured. Martinez didn't make it. We barely got away. She's in the back of the van sedated like we did her roommate. It'll be at least an hour before we get to the airport."

"Damn it! I told them the girl had help. We weren't prepared for them here and now there. Stone is on a war path. I think he wants to go after the people who helped her."

"Call me when you arrive at the airport. New York is a hop, skip and a jump to the Caribbeans.

"Everything happened so fast," said Jacob.

"Red doesn't know we have her."

"No worries, you have the prize. Let's keep it that way," said St. John.

"She's a high-profile public figure. I don't want her seen. She'll draw to much attention."

"If you haven't seen the news she's all over it."

"Can we get a ride to New York?" asked Jacob.

"We have instructions to meet a contact named Rhino. Our assignment is to find some girl named Darcy."

"Sure, no problem."

Richard called Jon.

"We have our sister and captured the guys watching our parents' home."

"I've extracted as much information as I could from them. I'm overnighting you their ID's, phones and the information they gave us via our special courier."

"We have one pit stop to make before leaving for New York. I'll be paying respects to an old friend at the cemetery."

tips

"I did get a couple of tips. Their command center is somewhere in Northern California."

"They're upset that they've lost so many men. I believe they'll be coming for you. I can't tell you where or when."

"I'm counting on that," said Jon.

"There's only a few places they can go."

"Do me a favor. Call Ryan," said Richard.

"See how he's doing?"

"He's expecting some old colleagues. They won't be showing up."

Jon called Ryan.

"Ryan, how's The Big Apple?"

"It never sleeps," he said.

"Funny you should call."

"Why is that?"

"Are you sitting down?"

"You are not going to believe who just called me."

Chapter 39

Wednesday
4:30 p.m. (PST)
Skaggs Island Naval Communication Station

Revenge

Stone's rage created a new mission. He ordered Slim to find out who helped the girl in Sacramento.

He made it clear in four words, "I want them dead."

His Information Technology crew of Slim, Jim and Jerry found the answer in the phone used to call Darcy.

It belonged to an Emily Rose-Xavier. Her last known address in Sacramento. There was something odd. The find me feature on her phone showed GPS coordinates somewhere in Lafayette, CA.

Ambrosia's phone had been disabled for days. Suddenly, it sprang to life. The GPS coordinates showed the same location, Lafayette, CA. Something's not adding up.

Slim and his crew worked throughout the day building a profile on Emily. By the end of the evening, they knew everything about her.

Her husband, Malcom Xavier was a wealthy real estate developer. They had twins, a boy and girl. Emily received her Ph.D. in Library Science from Florida State University and worked at a public library. Hacking her phone under her favorite contacts they discovered his phone number as well.

Red wanted to know more.

"Dig deeper on him," he said.

Red questioned Stone about his motivation. For obvious reasons he was hell bent on finding and eliminating their unknown adversaries.

They argued for nearly an hour going back and forth on their priorities. Red wanted to stick to their original objective. Capture girls for St. Jon's trafficking network. His logic: it was easy money.

Stone's warrior mentality and built-in rage couldn't let it go. He'd lost a lot of good soldiers. He wanted to find the missing girls and to avenge the lives of the men he'd lost. Blood ran through his eyes and created a shift in his priorities.

Slim caught a break. One of Malcom's telephone numbers went to a private security company. That became a problem. He couldn't find any information on it. It was there yet it wasn't. It was as if they were invisible. It was like hitting a brick wall.

Stone was sure they were the ones who intervened on the girls' abduction in Sacramento and Napa. His focus was to seek and destroy.

They found Malcom's net worth. He was worth billions.

Red thought for a while then said, "everybody hold up. This may be a golden opportunity."

"I want to know everything about him and what things are important to him."

"I want his security company out in the open."

"Let's see who these people really are," he said.

Chapter 40

Wednesday
5:30 p.m. (PST)
Skaggs Island Naval Communication Station

Good News, Bad News

Red, "you have a call coming in from Mr. St. John," said Slim.

Red answered with a dry, "yes."

"Did you hear the news?"

"What news?"

"Your boys got the girl!"

"What? What are you talking about?"

"I just got a call from Jacob. He said they got the girl, Ambrosia. They're on their way to the airport."

"I'm arranging transport at a small airport near Omaha. I'm sending her to the Caribbeans. Your men will be dropped off in New York to catch the runner Darcy."

"That's crazy. I talked to them an hour ago. They had the girl's parents. They were going to video tape extracting information from them on her whereabouts and send it to me."

"Our call dropped. I haven't been able to reconnect with them. I only get their voice mail."

"Tell me what you know?" asked Red.

Jacob told me, "when the girl showed up they went to grab her but ran into trouble. Martinez didn't make it."

"Hold on a second."

Red turned to Slim. "Call them."

Their phones went to voice mail.

He ordered Slim to trace their phones.

"Let's pinpoint their exact locations."

"Something's not making sense," said Red.

"What's not?" asked St. John.

"If the girl showed up they were to call me. But I haven't heard a word from them since then. My calls keep going to voice mail."

Boss, you gotta see this, said Slim."

Red walked to one of Slims computers. The GPS tracker showed their phones were not where they were supposed to be.

"I think we've got another problem," he said to St. John.

"And what's that?"

"I'm looking at the GPS coordinate's on their phones. Their phones are traveling west."

"What the hell are you talking about?"

I just talked to Jacob less than an hour ago."

"You said they were headed to Omaha. We are looking at their phones and they're moving west, way past Omaha. They're not answering my calls either. I'm going to follow their movement."

"Call them back. Maybe you'll have better luck than me."

St. John called Martinez's phone first. It went to an automated messaging system. He called Jacob but that call also went to voice mail.

He called Red and asked, "can you track Martinez's phone?"

"I called him twice and got nothing but a voice mail."

A few minutes later, Red called him back.

"We can't track his phone. His last known location is somewhere in Iowa."

"I don't like this," growled, Red.

St. John called his transport company.

"Wait an hour. If your passengers don't show, call me."

He made another call only to be interrupted by a call he didn't want.

"You fucked up!" said the caller.

"I know, I know but I'll make up for it."

"No and yes. You will make up for it but not now."

"We have a change in plans."

"I don't understand," said St. John.

"Shut up and listen!"

"Leave everything as it is unless you have a stroke of luck and can quietly capture Ambrosia. You and your cowboys screw up has given us a golden opportunity. The CMA is getting publicity we can't buy."

Chapter 41

Thursday
May 24, 2018
8:00 a.m.
Iowa

Invisible Securities

A nine-seater Lear jet landed at the small landing strip. Ambrosia and company quickly hopped on board, bound for New York.

11:30 a.m.
Northern California

Two telephones were delivered to a building in Lafayette, CA.

12:00 noon

Jon called Malcom.

"Pick up Emily. Get your kids as soon as possible. My people have eyes on you. Call me as soon as you have them. I'll give you the details later."

Malcom signaled to his partner Suzanne that he had an emergency.

Suzanne's phone rang.

Jon began to explain Malcom's weekend. Suzanne interrupted him— "tell me something I don't know."

"Your building is under surveillance. I'm not sure of their intentions."

"My people are in your lobby. They're dressed in ISC blue uniforms with their names and our IT logo."

"Tighten your security. I don't want a panic. I'll call you back when it's clear."

Suzanne sat and thought for a moment, a mystified look on her face. What the hell is going on?

She called her building security.

"Lock the building down. Be discreet and call me immediately if we have any unexpected visitors."

The phone rang at the business office of Muriel Seaborn, Principal Administrator at the Institute for Investment Education.

Jon was brief.

"Put the school on lockdown for the rest of the day. I already have people in the dorms doing janitorial work. They'll be wearing green uniforms with their names and ISC logos to identify themselves."

Momentarily stunned, she was curious and wanted to know more.

"Alexandria Middleton is a target for abduction. My people will protect her and the school. I'll call you when it is clear."

She knew of Invisible Securities, but up until now there was never a need for them. Now she felt the chill of an impending threat.

During the building construction Jon installed a special light in every classroom and on the school yard. It was only to be used in an emergency. This was one of those times.

Muriel hit the button. Throughout the campus red lights blinked on and off. Doors automatically closed in every part of the building. The school went into immediate lockdown.

12:23 p.m.

Malcom called Jon.

"I have everyone with me."

"What's going on!"

"Remember your act of good faith this weekend? Well, the guy who got away from the safe house is looking for revenge. You're now his target."

"He's coming after us?"

"Yes! He's a resourceful SOB. Emily's phone gave him a lot of information. He figured out who you and Emily are by hacking her phone. We captured several of his guys. After a little coaxing we gathered a ton of information We also got their phones."

"They know about us except who we are."

"I know everything about them except where they are."

"They're coming for us too. I just don't know where or when."

"We haven't identified their exact location yet, but we've been following them. They're digging deep on Emily."

"So, what's the plan? asked Malcom.

"Sun Tzu."

"The Art of War?"

"Yep."

"Remember his major tenets?"

"Yea, he had a lot. Which ones?"

"Secure yourself against defeat by defeating the enemy by his own hands."

"I have a spy in their camp."

"The second one: never fight a war on two fronts."

"He went after Ambrosia and lost that battle. Now they're coming after Emily and your family."

"I've anticipated that. I have plans for them that won't end well," said Jon.

Chapter 42

Home Sweet Home

We landed and taxied to a private hangar at Teterboro Airport, New Jersey.

Thrilled and eager to get to my apartment I could hardly contain myself. The sooner I got there the better. I wanted to be in my own bedroom, take a bath in my own tub, and change into my own clothes.

A black Lincoln Town Car with black tinted windows met us. Richard knew paparazzi's would be everywhere. Every precaution was made to ensure no one saw me until she arrived at her apartment. A small crowd of reporters stood standing outside. No questions were answered as Edward cleared the way into the building.

Upon arriving at the front desk, the security guard did a double take. It took her a minute to realize she was staring at me.

"Wow! It's been a while. You've changed," she said.

"We've been following you in the news."

"Yeah, I've been on the road. I lost the key to my apartment."

"It's okay, we've cleaned up your place and collected your mail."

"Mail? I have mail? I shouldn't have any. All my mail is directed to my office."

"My bad. You have junk mail. Your roommates have a week's worth. We have it stored in the mailroom. We'll bring it up shortly."

Richard stopped her.

"We'll come and get it."

He made it clear.

"We are not here," he told her.

When I entered my apartment, it looked staged. It felt awkward at first, but I relaxed once I entered my bedroom. It looked as I'd left it, just a little dusty.

I grabbed a key card and a door key from my dresser.

"I think we may want to change these."

I handed them to Richard.

Richard called Jon.

"We're here."

"Vanessa is on her way," he said.

The apartment phone rang. Edward answered and knocked on Ambrosia's door.

"You have a call."

"Hi, it's me," said Vanessa.

We both cried trying to talk at the same time.

"Are you alright, I asked."

"Yes and no. Physically I'm alright but I'm far from being alright."

"How are you?"

"I'm scared but home. My brothers are here."

"That's good. I'm with Nathan."

"He has a partner, Samantha, she's with us too."

"I'm coming home."

"Wait for me."

"I will."

"See you soon."

Chapter 43

2:00 p.m.
Manhattan, New York

The Deal

The Red Baron called Rhino.

"I need seven good men for tonight. I can pay them cash for one nights service."

"Can you handle that?" he asked.

"Sure, I can handle just about anything. But with this kind of notice it's gonna cost you."

"How much are we talking?" asked Red.

"What's the job?"

"I need to take down a high-end adversary."

"Hmmm, you're not saying much," said Rhino.

"Let me see if I got this. You have a hig-end target for tonight with no details. That's a problem. I'm gonna have to get back to you on that. I'm guessing $10,000 a man."

"What! Seventy grand!" exclaimed Red. "That's expensive!"

"Whoa! You want seven of my best men for a high-risk job, tonight for which you've given me no detailed information on the target? You of all people know I don't work like that."

"If you want my men you're gonna have to pay for it, all up front in cash. Otherwise, this conversation is over."

"Hold on a sec! I've got a couple of things going on that can make us a lot more money," said Red.

"Go on."

"My target is a super wealthy real estate developer's wife. I plan on kidnapping her. We can extract a significant ransom from her husband. The problem I have is there's a private security firm that provides them with round the clock protection. I've got to take them out of the picture tonight! The ransom will be in the millions. I can get you half the money now and the other half when the deal is done," said Red.

"Wait a minute! Now you want me to send my men up against a high-end security firm? Now, you're adding kidnapping and maybe murder that I'll have to clean up?" Nah, I'm not feeling this. My men won't either.

He made a counteroffer of $100,000 up front and 20% of the ransom."

"Rhino, you're killing me."

"Don't fuck with me or I will."

"I know, I know! I got it. Give me an hour. I'll have the money. Deal?"

"Yeah, deal. I'll call you tonight at twenty-one hundred hours. Send me the details. I'll pass it on to my contact. The lead guy goes by the handle, the Ghost. Bring the cash or he's out"

"By the way, what happened to New York? I'm sitting here on my ass thinking you were going to call me with an assignment. Now, you're calling me with this shit.

"I know you and the Enforcer have been into human trafficking. You know that's not my thing."

"Sorry for the misunderstanding. I have a high-level contractor who wants me to find a girl in up-state New York. It's all connected. When we finish all of this we'll meet in the Bahamas. I'm overdue for a vacation. We'll sit on a beach drinking Mai Tai's and counting money. I'll tell you the whole story. Trust me, this guy is worth billions."

"Trust you my ass. I'll believe it when I see it."

"Don't be late!"

Chapter 44

4:45 p.m. (EST)
New York

Coming Home

A plane landed at LaGuardia Airport and taxied to a U.S. Customs checkpoint. Before anyone departed, a messenger delivered a package for Special Agent Nathan Gilbert.

The customs agent inspected the plane. The arrivals matched its manifest. Three members of the flight crew and three passengers. Upon seeing the FBI ID's, he gave the package to Nathan. Courtesy of a request from Samantha was Vanessa's ID, passport, and the keys to her apartment.

When they got to the apartment complex the security guard smiled and said, "welcome home."

"Your roommate and guests are upstairs waiting for you."

Vanessa entered her apartment and ran into my arms. We fell into a long series of hugs, cries, and laughter. After gathering our composure, we made introductions.

Samantha looked at Richard.

"I know you," Richard grinned

"Well, I'll be damn, Samantha Jackson!

"It's been a while," he said.

Nathan and Edward shook hands, bewildered. Questions filled each of their minds.

Our apartment's phone rang, I answered. It was building security.

"You have a visitor. A Mr. Ryan Norris is here to see Richard Alexander. What do you want me to do?"

I looked at Richard. He gave me a nod of approval.

"Send him up," I said.

Ryan entered, a concerned look on his face.

He embraced Richard and shook hands with everyone.

"What's wrong?" asked Richard.

"As I came into the building, I got a strange feeling. Two guys looked out of place. That's not normal around here. People who live in this neighborhood have things to do, places to go. These guys didn't fit. They were standing on opposite corners observing the building."

I caught him staring at me.

"Is this what all the fuss is about?" he said.

"I shot back, what's that supposed to mean?"

"I've seen your photos. You look different. I been a bodyguard for a lot of people, especially beautiful women.

Even with your change I didn't expect to see someone as beautiful as you."

"I apologize if my comment offended you."

Richard quickly intervened.

"Ambrosia, this is Ryan Norris. The boss sent him. He's gonna be your personal bodyguard."

"We were on the same Navy Seal team. After he got out of the war he became a professional cage fighter. He's a human self-defense weapon. He specializes in guarding rich and famous high-profile celebrities."

"Don't let his good looks and manners fool you. He's one of the most dangerous men on the earth. I wouldn't want to tangle with him in a dark alley."

"Man, that last fight was crazy. I couldn't believe you gave up your career after that. You guys should have seen it. It was one hell of a fight."

"No wonder people call you Rhino. You're a beast. I thought for sure you'd be the next world heavyweight champion."

"After that fight, I got a call from Jon. He made me an offer I couldn't refuse. I thought long and hard about his offer. Now, I get to use my skills, but I don't have to think about concussions, dental work, or health insurance. Besides, the pay and living conditions are way better," said Ryan.

Ryan knelt on one knee, bowed his head, extending his hand.

"Ms. Alexander, I am humbly at your service."

I smiled, extending my hand.

"Thank you."

He held my hand a bit longer than he should have.

"Ryan, remember your assignment," cracked Edward as he laughed out loud.

"Don't forget she's our baby sister. You're just to be her bodyguard."

Ryan stood quickly and changed subjects.

"Our abductors are getting an introduction to The Ghost tonight."

"That should be fun," quipped Richard.

"Okay, enough with the drama," said Vanessa.

"I need a shower and to get outta these clothes."

"I want some tea but there's nothing here. Starbucks is a few blocks from here."

She went to her room. Twenty minutes later she came out dressed in a low V-cut blouse, skinny jeans, and tennis shoes—all black. She put on a New York Mets baseball cap and dark Oakley sunglasses. She headed for the door when Richard stopped her.

"Hold on a second. If you're going out you'll need company," said Richard.

"Any volunteers?"

"We've got grocery shopping to do. Why don't Vanessa and I go for a walk?" said Edward.

"This apartment complex is not at full capacity. I'll bet a dollar there are a few vacant furnished units available. I'll check that out," said Richard.

Ryan replied, "my gut tells me I'm not going anywhere. Besides, I've got to follow up on my west coast adventure."

"Let's meet back her at 7:30 p.m. for dinner. We've got a lot to talk about," said Richard.

"We're already on the modeling agency but we don't have jurisdiction on foreign soil," said Nathan.

Make
"Samantha, can we contact with those people you talked about earlier?"

"Sure, that's an easy one," she said.

"They're standing in this room."

Chapter 45

6:30 p.m.
New York

Ryan Norris

Ambrosia came out of her room and quietly sat on the couch next to Ryan. His conversation was intense. He nearly jumped to the ceiling when he turned and saw me.

Caught by surprised he hung up and gathered himself. He had to be slipping, he thought to himself.

"How are you?" he asked.

"I'm feeling a little safer."

As for the call he'd clearly been on, I asked, what was that all about?"

"We're about to deal with the people in California who came after you. We're also working on a plan for that boat. Can I do anything for you?"

"No, not now. I'm tired and restless but can't sleep. I thought of going for a walk, but I know that's out of the question. My walls were closing in on me. I came out here to think."

"Think about what?"

"This whole mess," I said running agitated fingers through my hair. "You, my brothers, your organization."

"I can't seem to wrap my brains around any of this."

"Everything was going so well. This all seems so...surreal."

"I can't stop asking myself, why am I taking my company public?" All of this has got to have something to do with it, but I can't put my finger on anything tangible."

"I don't know much about your business. My job is intelligence gathering and protection. I'm good at that," Ryan said.

"I know we're getting close to finding this St. John guy. But the boat thing tells me this is bigger than him. If I ever run into him..."

He stopped himself mid-sentence.

"I shouldn't say anything else."

"I hope you do catch him. I only met him for a minute."

"He's handsome, smooth, and very scary. People like him that sour our business. Women in my line of work, especially women must be careful around men," I said.

"Men tend to get sexually aggressive when they're drinking and doing drugs around beautiful women. They feed off each other's ego. Their testosterone gets up when there's a lot of them and only a few women."

"That's the reason I started my company. I grew tired of the sexual advances. I wanted control over my own environment."

186

"I feel you. That's the reason I take jobs like this."

"I hate those guys. They act like fools around beautiful women."

"I'm curious about something."

"What's the first thing that pops into your brain when you see a beautiful woman?" asked Ambrosia

"It's a long story," he said.

"I'm not going anywhere."

"I joined the navy at 18. I applied for Seal training at 20. We went through 24 weeks of Basic Underwater Demolition/SEAL school and 28 weeks of SEAL qualification training. Our first deployment was a training exercise that lasted 30 months. We rarely saw women. When they cut us loose we were wild as bucking broncos. Drinking and sex was all we thought about. It took me a while to mature."

"To mature?"

"I met Richard in Seal Training. He left after 6 years; I left four years later. After touring the Middle East, Afghanistan, and Iraq, I saw a lot of female abuse. The first job I took was a bouncer at an exotic dance club in LA."

"I got to take my aggression out on silly bastards who think of women as pleasure instruments. I loved kicking their ass. That led me to cage fighting, body building and guarding celebrities."

"I've had my share of affairs. I even fell in love once. When she broke my heart, I lost my trust in women."

"You still haven't answered my question."

He walked to the window. Time stood still as he gazed at the sunset gathering his thoughts.

"When I see a beautiful woman the first thing I try to do is look past her physical appearance. I look for beauty that comes from her heart."

"I've seen all sides. Beautiful women who use their beauty to take advantage of poor saps like me. Others who get their hearts broken by jerks who are only out to get laid."

"A few get lucky and find a lifetime friend."

"I've learned sex is a twenty-minute exercise, but a friendship lasts a lifetime."

"So, you've never been married?"

"Do you have children?"

"Oh, I've been married, twice."

"They married me because I could take care of them, but they didn't love me. It bummed me out. I walked away because God only knows what I'm capable of doing."

"If I had a kid, out there somewhere , it would be news to me, as no one has come forward claiming 'I Am The Father.' How about you?"

"I married once. He cheated on me. He couldn't keep his cloths on. He claimed our industry had too many sexually aggressive women coming after him all of the time. He couldn't control himself."

Before she could finish her tale of marital woe, Nathan and Samantha entered. They were all excited about something but wanted to wait for the others to return before they got into a conversation.

A few minutes later, Vanessa came in with both Edward and Richard. They brought groceries and dinner.

"That was some walk!" Edward said first.

"You were right. Two guys were surveilling the building."

" The guys followed us to Starbucks. The place was packed. We were standing shoulder to shoulder. The line went out the door. While we were waiting for her tea, one of the guys came in. He made a judgement error and went to the bathroom. I followed him. He turned his back on me and never saw what came next. Anyway, I got his ID and his phone."

"I called Richard. He showed up as we were coming out of the coffee shop. We went for dinner at the gourmet grocery store around the corner. The other guy made a mistake by following us to closely. Richard stepped out of sight near the alley behind the Sheraton and grabbed him. I'm not sure what Richard did."

"He was too easy, said Richard. They'll find him in the dump when they empty the truck that picks up trash from those big green garbage containers. I got his phone and ID too."

"We'll send their phones to Jon. He'll run their ID's through the system. I already know what they'll find; ex-military."

Changing subjects Richard said, "I found two furnished vacant units. One is down the hall. The other is a floor below."

"Edward and I are taking the one down the hall. Tomorrow we're having cameras installed at each end of the hallway. Our cameras will cover areas where the complex doesn't have eyes."

"The bureau has its own houses but being close is a better option. We'll explore that tomorrow," said Nathan.

We ate, poured wine when the conversation turned to the investigation.

"Nathan shared his excitement.

"We got the telephone records of the CMA for the past three months."

"We've identified several people who may be accomplices in our investigation. Our agents are currently digging into their details," said Samantha.

Ryan brought them up to date about activities on the west coast.

"I told Jon about the boat. He normally doesn't get involved in our work."

"I don't know why but he's taking a personal interest in this. He said he'll work on that when he's finished tonight."

"What about Gabriel and Darcy?" asked Vanessa.

"The three of us have discussed Gabriel. He's a jet setting playboy," I said.

"All he thinks about is money."

"He was upset when we didn't support his IPO. But he's got Jeremy and Paul wrapped around the idea that going public would make them wealthy."

"I got on his bad side. He couldn't seduce me. He tried several times and failed."

"Paul is another one. He was disappointed he wasn't included as a primary investor. He backed off once I explained to him that he was not an initial investor. He seemed to settle down when I told him he'd be included in the Employee Stock Option Plan."

"Some of the executive staff complained too. I told them the same thing. They had no skin in the company."

"The primary investors are going to be in the first position. After that all of our initial stock will be released to the secondary market. A lot of them didn't like that so I wouldn't count any of them out."

"I need to warn you. There are secret affairs going on in the company. I'm not supposed to know but I can put two and two together. No one talks about it, but I see and hear things. I haven't done anything yet, but I'm going to real soon."

Ambrosia called Darcy. She wasn't expecting her to answer, but did upon hearing my voice.

"Where are you?" she asked.

"I finally made it home. Vanessa is here too."

"Our brothers are with us. I've even got a personal bodyguard. It's safe for you to come home."

Darcy's response surprised me.

"I don't know if it's wise. After Saturday morning I think someone will be coming after me. I know too much."

I put her on speaker.

"Our brothers are here. We have the FBI and a private security company."

Nathan spoke first.

"Darcy, it's me Nathan. What's going on?"

"Gabriel or someone he works with wants me dead.

I'm not sure who to trust."

"Darcy, it's Richard."

"I promise you, we can and will protect you, but you need to do exactly what I tell you."

"Go to an ATM. Withdraw as much cash as you can. Use the cash to buy two burner phones. Call the apartment and give Ambrosia a location far from where you'll actually be. Dump your phone there. Call me with the first burner phone from a place with a lot of people. I will set up a place where it will be safe to get you home."

"Correction, we'll bring you home safely. I'll be there too," I said.

Chapter 46

Thursday
5:20 p.m. PST
Skaggs Island Naval Communication Station
California

Surprise, Surprise

"Stone, I spoke with Rhino. He wants $100,000 plus 20% of the ransom or we get no support personnel. I'm looking at $120,000 in cash right now. We have more in our offshore accounts. If this guy is as rich as you say he is we'll squeeze him for millions."

"Where are you now?" asked Red.

"I'm reconning the wife. We'll take her after dusk."

6:30 p.m.
Sacramento, CA

Stone and Jim drove to their first recon site. The Sacramento South Pocket Public Library.

Jim noted, "If she gets off at seven, why is a Sacramento Police cruiser parked out front?"

"Good question."

"Let's check out the other site."

Their house was in the middle of a small, gated community. It had one main street, no sidewalks and a couple of side streets.

"Looks like we got two entry options," said Jim.

"We can comb through the directory and push buttons hoping someone will let us in, or we can wait for someone to come in or out."

"I'm opting for following someone through. Circle the block. Let's see what's on the other side."

There was another entry gate. They drove from one gate to another several times. Finally, they parked across the street from the gate with the most amount of traffic.

A car drove up and entered. They followed it in. A red Camaro was parked in the driveway. The interior house lights were on.

Stone surmised, "we must have missed them coming in from the other side."

"This is an active neighborhood," said Jim.

As they spoke, people were walking dogs with a few kids riding bicycles and playing street soccer.

For the next three hours they drove, ate dinner, and sat watching and waiting. A series of UPS, Fed X and Amazon delivery vans came back and forth.

The neighborhood quieted at sunset.

9:30 p.m.

They grew impatient and decided to follow a white delivery van through the gate.

Jim noted, "it's kind of late for an evening delivery." His partner agreed.

"I don't like this", said Stone. Be ready to move."

Jim nodded, already thinking the same thing.

The van stopped one house before their target. A woman hopped out and disappeared into the back. They drove around it to get a better view. The driveway faced the mouth of a cul-de-sac where a black Range Rover sat down the street. They passed the house when another white van came up and slowly crossed over the middle of the street heading right towards them.

Stone realized it was a trap and yelled for Jim to get them out of there.

Jim slammed on the gas pedal and drove around the truck making tracks across a neighbor's lawn. The truck tried to cut them off but missed. They sideswiped it and sped down the street smashing through a black rod iron gate as it was closing. That slowed them down when the black Range Rover appeared on their bumper. Jim made a right turn towards Pocket Road. He attempted to turn left at a stop sign but several speeding cars cut him off forcing him to turn right when the chasing SUV rammed him.

Jim sped a quarter mile down the street. Stone pulled out a nine-millimeter with a silencer attached. He fired at the weaving Range Rover several times but missed.

Jim ran a red light nearly crashing into a car making a left turn. He zigzagged around it and broadsided several parked cars. Stone fired more shots, all misses.

He raced around a curve in the road running a stop sign. The red Camaro smashed into the tail end of his car. Both cars spun out of control jumping the curb and coming to rest on the grass at Garcia Bend Park.

Air bags exploded into their faces breaking Jim's nose. Stone was pinned in his seat and struggled to get free. He managed to open the door and crawled out. While on his hands and knees, he looked for his handgun. He stood when a woman call his name. Instinctively, he turned to face her and took the full force of an ARMA-100 Bean Bag.

The gut shot slammed him into the opened car door and he fell to the ground. He staggered trying to get up when another bean bag hit him in the face. The woman made sure he was down by knocking him unconscious with the butt of her rifle.

Before he could react, Jim saw the red laser of EC's weapon pointed at his head. He crawled out with one hand raised in surrender, the other hand holding his bleeding nose. EC struck him with his gun. The two were dragged into the Range Rover.

They left the scene as neighbors poured out of their homes to see what was happening. All they saw, however, was the wreckage. Sirens were heard as a small crowd gathered. In the dark of the night, the crowd missed seeing the tail end of a large black car speeding towards the Interstate.

Chapter 47

The Break-In

Slim's GPS tracker traced all of the phones to an address in Lafayette, CA. It was a large grey four-story building with no distinguishing features. Located off a dead-end road, its only identification was the number 1 painted on the building's exterior.

Red and Jerry scoured the building looking for security cameras, entry and exit points. They observed a small parking lot and a driveway leading to an underground parking garage.

"If they have surveillance cameras they're well-hidden," noted Red. "Do you see any?"

"Nope," said Jerry, looking at his laptop, I'm only picking up some cars in the underground garage. Several lights are on inside the front door and in the upper offices. I don't see a power generator either. For a building this size there's gotta be a big one."

His meeting with The Ghost was in the parking lot adjacent to a recently closed building on Via Roble Road. On their approach Red saw several parked cars and a lone man.

The Ghost, a big man who stood 6' 8". He was armed and dressed in black camouflage and a black ski mask. All you could see were his eyes. He blinked a neon flashlight motioning Red to him.

Red got out and cautiously made introductions. He felt he'd met him somewhere a long time ago and asked if their paths had ever crossed before.

The Ghost didn't answer the question, but asked one of his own.

"What do you have?"

Red pulled out blueprints of the building. They contained little information about its interior.

"I've got details from Rhino. We did our homework too," said The Ghost.

He pulled out schematics of the building.

"I have info on its interior and all its entry and exit points."

"The money?" The Ghost asked.

Jerry pulled a duffle bag from the back seat. A man stepped out of the dark. He was dressed identical to The Ghost. He took the bag, opening, and inspecting it. With a nod of approval, The Ghost raised his fist. Five men appeared out of nowhere. All were heavily armed and also dressed in the same black camouflage.

Red was impressed. He knew how Rhino worked. His intel said they operated in the shadows. You'd never see them come or go. As he huddled under a lamplight he complemented The Ghost.

"I knew you guys were good, but I didn't know you'd be that good."

Ignoring the complement, The Ghost walked him through the building layout.

"The building is an electronic monster," said Jerry.

"From what I see there's a lot of heat coming from the fourth floor in the back. It's connected to a series of communication dishes and antennas on the roof."

"The readings I'm getting are off the charts, but the signals are blocked. I'm getting nothing but electronic static interference and heatwaves."

"My body sensors are picking up people. One near the front door and some on the third floor. The weirdest thing is the underground parking garage. There's a zone where I'm getting nothing. Just empty space. It may be a vault or something."

The Ghost asked Red how he wanted to proceed?

"I want to commandeer the building and sweep it floor by floor, room by room. I wanna know everything about it; it's operations and whatever else is going on inside."

"I've lost a lot of men this week. This is the closest thing we've got in tracking down whoever is behind it. Some of my men are still missing. I want confirmation that they're either dead or alive."

"My tracer says all of the missing phones are on the third floor. I'm not sure of their exact location," said Jerry.

"Go quietly," said Red.

"I have no problems with collateral damage. "If we can take anyone alive it'll be a gift."

The Ghost pointed to two men and barked orders.

"Secure the perimeter. We'll take the entry and go room by room, one floor at a time. We'll meet in the lobby at 2400 hours," he said.

The Ghost handed com links to Red and Jerry.

Jerry suggested cutting the power and flushing them out whoever was inside, he said."

"It doesn't seem to be that many people in the building."

Red gave The Ghost a disgusting look and shook his head.

"These are security people," he said. "If they're as good as they've been I don't want to alert them to our presence. I want to surprise them like they've done us. I'm going to disable their operations and destroy the building."

"Jerry, stay here and monitor any movement outside. I don't want anyone snicking up behind me."

"We clear soldier?"

"Yes sir!"

They waited until they were assured the perimeter was clear and proceeded through heavy glass doors leading into a large lobby. The doors were not locked. A lone guard stood behind a counter in the lobby.

Red sensed this is too easy.

He fell back saying, "I'll cover you guys."

Without hesitation The Ghost shot the security guard and pointed to his team.

"Start room by room from here. Work your way up. When you're done we'll meet back here."

He and his men split up and disappeared into the building.

Red's eyes darted back and forth as he stood at the entrance. He walked up and down a quiet lobby surveying everything. He turned to the counter where the guard was shot. There was no body.

Suddenly, the lobby went pitch black followed by one sound, a loud click at the entry.

He ran to the door. It was locked. He shot the door. His bullets ricocheted off the bullet proof glass. He hit his comm link to talk. He got nothing.

A voice called out.

"Roger Berryman. Or should I call you Sargent Major Berryman?"

He turned around and around looking for the voice.

Gun fire rang out.

Red was hit in his gun hand, then his left shoulder, right knee, and left hip.

The lights came on as the shooter stood over him, removing his mask.

Red realized he'd been betrayed.

"You," he whimpered, seeing the face of The Ghost.

Jon cracked his skull with the butt of his gun.

Chapter 48

Friday
May 25, 2018
9:45 a.m. (EST)
Manhattan, New York

The Arrival

The CMA staff assembled for their end of the week meeting.
Paul Gregory opened with the introduction of CMA's new
Chief of Public Relations, Katherine Weinstein.

The press had been parked outside their building for
days breathlessly waiting to get comments.

CMA remained front page news.

To combat fake news, Katherine established
scheduled briefings at 10:15 a.m. and 1:45 p.m. This would
give the press ample time to prepare their stories for the
afternoon and evening broadcasts.

She'd put together morning briefing documents and
was preparing to meet the press when a black limousine
pulled up.

Ryan stepped out followed by Richard and Edward.
They cleared a path for Samantha, Vanessa and I as we were
ushered into the building.

The waiting crowd went nuts. Reporters yelled
questions as photographers created a symphony with
nonstop clicking of their cameras.

Paul was going over the weekend things to-do-checklist when an uproar came from the outer office.

When I entered, the staff dropped everything and ran to me. It was a love fest of hugs and kisses.

Jeremy came out of his office only to be met by Nathan and Samantha. He'd barely said hello when Samantha jammed her finger into his chest and ordered him back into his office.

"We have to talk!" she said.

Monique ran to me giving me a long hug.

"You colored your hair. I like the cut. I'm so happy to see you," she said.

Paul was speechless.

He gave Vaness and I welcome back hugs.

Behind her stood three men.

"And who might these gentlemen be?" Paul asked.

"These are my brothers, Richard and Edward Alexander."

Ryan Norris introduced himself.

"I'm Rhino Norris, Ambrosia's personal bodyguard."

"Anywhere she goes, I go."

Katherine introduced herself.

"I'm your new public relations director" Katherine said by way of a greeting. It's an honor to meet the two of you."

"I'm glad you're here. Your timing is perfect."

"Can I speak with you two for a moment, privately."

"Give them a minute to get settled. They've had a rough week," said Paul.

Dismissing him as a non-entity Katherine ignored him and his comment, continuing on as if he hadn't said a word.

"It's important I speak with you two now," she said to Ambrosia and Vanessa.

"I have a scheduled press conference at 10:15. Please follow me. I promise this won't take long."

"Before we go my brothers need a place to work. Preferably a private office," I said.

"Sure, They can use Darcy's office," said Paul.

"Where do you want me?" asked Ryan.

"Out front. I don't want any uninvited guests coming in.

"Monique, please make arrangements for Mr. Norris."

"Done. Can I get you anything?" she asked.

"Nope, I'm good for now."

Paul called everyone back into the conference room to finish their meeting. Vanessa and I joined them after meeting with Chief Weinstein.

In my presence, Paul had trouble speaking. After 10 minutes I grew frustrated listening to him bumble his way through the meeting.

I took control, asking questions on everything I'd missed since I've been gone.

I informed them of my successful Dog and Pony Show presentations to institutional and private investors.

"I've got $30 million in funding commitments."

"We are going to be the game changer in the modeling business."

"We are going to blow the competition away, and all of you are going to be a part of it!"

My comments were met with thunderous applause.

Chapter 49

6:30 a.m. (PST)
Skaggs Island Naval Communication Station
Vallejo, California

Captured

For once in many months Slim slept peacefully without interruption. Eleven hours had passed since he'd spoken to either Red or Stone. With all of his sophisticated technology he couldn't find them.

He headed towards the outer doors to get some much-needed fresh air. He reached to unlock the door.

An explosion sent him flying across the room, knocking him to the floor. Before he could gather himself a magnesium-based pyrotechnic bomb exploded.

He became conscious in a room surrounded by armed men. He and Jim were strapped in chairs looking up at Red, Jerry, Rafael, and Stone. They were all hanging upside down, facing each other near the floor.

The rags stuffed in their mouths were removed.

Stone struggled in his bindings. He tried to spit at anyone close to him. His reward, a swift kick to the face.

Red tried to whisper something. Wounded and bandaged from head to toe he could only mumble.

Jon strolled into the room.

Stone saw his face.

"Jon Johnston, he yelled as the man walked pass him. I should have known. You work for that double-crossing bastard Rhino!"

Jon turned back to him and kicked him in the back of his neck.

"You have it backwards. Ryan works for me. Unlike you, he's one of the good guys."

Jon slowly walked around the room assessing each one of the captives.

"I have a one-time offer," he said. "Anyone want to come work for me?"

"All you have to do is tell me everything about this Mr. St. John and his human trafficking network."

"Fuck you and that double-crossing bastard Rhino. We ain't telling you shit," said Stone.

"You know Corporal Phillips. I've heard someone use that line before."

"Do you remember Angel Martinez?"

"Angel? That overconfident prick. He's going to burn in hell just like you; you son of a bitch!"

Jon remained calm and said, "hell is not hot enough for you."

He pulled out a nine-millimeter Sig.

"Sex trafficking is an immortal sin. My wife was a victim of being trafficked in Africa. I saved her but I couldn't help many of her friends. I promised her I would never let that happen again."

"Corporal Phillips, you've been bad. You're responsible for sending innocent people into reprehensible situations. For that your penalty is..."

The back of Stone's head splattered, finishing Jon's sentence and, well...Stone.

Jon's demeanor changed in an instant.

"I am so sorry fellas." he said as if he hadn't just ended a man's life.

"I really feel bad about all this."

"Sargent Berryman or should I call you Red? I understand you're the leader of this outfit," he said gesturing toward the restrained men.

"I don't like you or your kind. Human trafficking and sexually slavery is disgustingly repulsive."

"I wanted to kill you back in Lafayette, but my kind heart overwhelmed me."

"My people worked hard patching you up. I wanted you alive so we could have an adult conversation."

"Should I start with you or with the others?"

Jon turned to Rafael. It seemed there was no honor among thieves. In the end it was every man for himself.

"Let's start with you then."

Rafael looked over to Red.

He gave no response, just shook his head and gave Jon a look that was equally repugnant and defiant.

Jon took a deep breath and fired. The top of Rafael exploded all over everyone.

Jerry spoke. Not wanting to be next.

"We're IT guys. We don't know much. We just follow orders."

"You're telling me you're an IT guy and you don't know shit?"

"Really!" Jerry shook his head. "We don't know anything," he said, his voice full of fear and distain.

Jon took another deep and breath and another shot.

"Somebody better talk to me. "I'm running out of patience fellas. "Speak your piece or rest in peace," he said.

"Wait, wait," sputtered, Jim. What do you wanna know?"

"Everything! I want to know every stinking detail about this whole operation. Don't try to play me. If I even think you're withholding something it won't end well."

Jim said, "We've got something better looking over at Slim.

"Tell him! his partner implored. "For God's sake tell him everything we've got!"

"We've recorded everything for the past seven years," Slim let out.

"You can have it all," he said.

"Everything? What's everything?" asked Jon.

"Everything. We've got contact names, dates, locations, telephone numbers, conversations and a lot of banking information," Slim said bargaining for his life.

"They were raping women, killing people, and selling humans like animals. We knew it was bad when they started laughing about it. We weren't into that."

"Yeah, they became uncontrollable," said Jim.

"They didn't know it, but we knew this day was coming," said Slim.

"We decided to secretly record their every move."

"We knew who they talked to and what they talked about," he continued. "We've collected offshore bank accounts and all of their accounting records. We started collecting St. John's information when we left Afghanistan."

"St. John's doesn't know it but once I got one of his wire transfers, I tricked him into opening a false file. It contained a trojan horse that gave me access to everything inside his system. I installed a keylogger program that recorded his every keystroke. I can control his phones and his computers anytime I want," said Slim.

"Whenever he communicated with his banks or his people I captured everything. I've got his passwords and security authentications," he said.

"We have world-wide access to all of his accounts, on and offshore," said Jim. "We've collected data on his sex trafficking activities including who and where his people are."

"I even know where 99 percent of his money is," said Slim. He has more than $250 million stashed around the world."

"I've got records the IRS, FBI, CIA, DIA, and NSA would love to see," said Slim, his voice somewhere between bragging and begging.

I can even tell you when and where his next auctions are going to be held."

"And why should I trust you?" asked Jon.

"We never really liked those guys."

"At first it was easy money."

"I took what the military's been using for years. All I needed was money to fund my own system."

"When we started working with St. John, we used his money and our military contacts to build a quantum computer system. I have zero-day vulnerability and remote access tools the public doesn't even know exists."

"If you have anything electronic or digital, I can hack it, eavesdrop on it, steal and record it without you knowing I was there."

"I even found your building."

"I tried using every phishing, spoofing, and spamming technology. I still couldn't get past your firewalls or break your encrypted messaging system."

"I never told them about your system. Your system is superior to anything I've seen. Whatever you have it's really good."

"When we left Iraq, me and Jim wanted out."

"Stone got pissed and started treating us like dogs."

"Red made us his indentured servants."

"Yeah, we became nothing more than paid slaves," said Jim

"Stone threatened to kill us and our entire families if we even thought about leaving. We didn't have much of a choice," said Slim.

"You can have it all. I'll show you how it all works."

"Please don't kill me!" begged Slim.

"This information is where?"

"It's in our building next door. It's our command and communications center."

Jim spoke up. "Can I ask you something?"

"What?"

"Does your offer still stand?"

"I can't speak for Slim, but I would love to work for you."

"Include me in on that," said Slim.

"For the last time, how can I trust you?"

"Cut me loose and let me see that gun," said Slim.

After cutting him from his chair, Jon removed the clip leaving him one shell and handed him the gun.

Slim walked over to Red and lifted his chin high enough to look into his eyes.

"This is for my family asshole," he said before pointing the gun at Red's forehead and pulling the trigger.

With the deed done he handed Jon his gun.

"Now, let's go get that bastard," he said.

Ten minutes later the ISC cleaners and IT teams entered the building. They left the compound clean. You'd never knew anyone was ever there.

Chapter 50

10:30 a.m. (EST)
Cosmopolitan Modeling Agency
Manhattan, New York

Revelations

"You lied to us the last time we were here," said Samantha.

That statement caught Jeremy by surprise.

"Excuse me!" he said.

"You know we've been investigating the internal operations of your company," said Nathan.

"You said you spent last weekend alone. You want to tell us the truth now?"

Jeremy's eyes were glued to the floor and when he spoke, his voice quivered, barely audible.

"Okay, yes, I was with someone," he admitted.

"We know that. We know who she is and how long she was there. The question is why'd you lie?"

"I lied because of the IPO."

"And?" asked Samantha.

"We have a conflict-of-interest policy that does not permit members of the Board or the Executive staff having interpersonal relationships with other members of our agency."

"Ambrosia was adamant about the policy."

"Sex scandals are widespread in our industry. She didn't want anyone using their positions of power to extract sexual favors from the staff or our contractual employees. It is a zero-tolerance policy with grounds for immediate termination."

"If word got out our careers here would be over. I'd lose everything."

"You mean to tell us you risked your company over a piece of ass?" asked Samantha.

"It's something that happened. We fell in love. We knew what it meant if we were caught."

"It gets worse. There's more. Are you ready?" asked Nathan.

The color disappeared from Jeremy's face.

"Oh God, what else could there be?"

"You have a rogue employee inside your agency," said Nathan.

"We've been going through your company telephone records. The main number from the switch board was used to cancel Ambrosias' credit cards and to shut down her phone."

"We don't know who, but the calls are linked to the people who kidnapped my sister and their failed attempts to capture Ambrosia," said Nathan.

"That same phone number tracks to conversations with a group that hacked Darcy's phone. They've been tracking her since her disappearance."

"We believe she's another target but she's smart and constantly on the move to stay one step ahead of them."

"They've never been able to pinpoint her exact location. Since then, we've neutralized their threat. We're bringing her home soon."

"Who has the authority to close company accounts?" asked Samantha.

Jeremy told the agent that other than himself and Ambrosia, Paul was the only other person with such authorization. But he'd still need prior approval from the Board."

"You don't delegate that function?" asked Nathan.

"Only Monique. She has limited authority, but she'd need one of us to signoff. To date we've never had an issue."

"Do you know of anyone who may have a vendetta against your company?" asked Samantha.

"Look, if you're asking if people are unhappy about the way things are run around here. Yes, they are. They'd have to get in line. I've learned one thing in this business. You can't please everyone. I've told the staff on many different occasions to come see me if they had an issue. No one has come to me yet."

"I admit there was a lot of discontent when the executive staff discovered they were excluded from being in on the primary offering of the IPO."

"Once we told them of the Employee Stock Option Plan, things settled down...or so I thought."

"You're lucky on one count," said Samantha.

"What's that?"

"You're not a person of interest."

"Where does that leave Anjelica and I?," voicing his lover's name out loud.

"Cooperate. Help us flush out the mole and maybe we'll turn a blind eye on your 'interpersonal relationship.'"

"I don't want her getting hurt."

"Then we have a deal?" asked Nathan.

"Yes, we do."

"They got up to leave when Samantha advised in a whisper that Anjelica break her modeling contract and marry him ASAP to avoid any repercussion of violating the company's non-fraternization policy."

"They found Richard and Edward in Darcy's office."

"Did you get all of that?"

"Yep, every word."

"Time to dig deeper."

Chapter 51

Friday, May 25, 2018
11:00 a.m. (PST)
Lafayette, CA

Inside Information

Jon was impressed and intrigued. After studying the details of information in Slim's database, he realized he was looking through doors few people had stepped through.

The information he took from Slim's computer system provided insight and a deep perspective on the inner operations of a worldwide human trafficking network and prostitution ring.

St. John had a global network. With more than $250 million in banks worldwide, he controlled a vast payroll of clients ranging from high-ranking company executives, law enforcement personnel, elected officials, and powerful members of the judiciary.

His payroll included a group of military veterans who operated his acquisition and disposal units. He controlled a fragmented union of pimps and enforcers that ran many local operations. All of the evidence was right in front of him.

This created a severe problem. Blowing their cover and exposing them would put innocent people in danger. These people would stop at nothing to prevent their secrets from getting out.

Jon decided on a slow delicate approach. He'd start by leaking a little bit of information at different time intervals. He'd start with the FBI.

He called Samantha.

"Adam Chandler's drowning was no accident. He was murdered. According to Slim's recorded conversations, a scuba diver pulled him underwater. His waders were filled with rocks. His body is somewhere a mile downstream from his fishing spot. He'll be in 60 feet of water. He may never be found unless a drought causes the river to run low."

"I'm sending an anonymous tip to the FBI office in New York. Helen Grace didn't die of food poisoning. They need to redo the tox report. They should look for Novichok. It's difficult to detect but it's a highly toxic nerve agent used in the Eastern Bloc countries to quietly eliminate rivals. It causes paralyses in breathing and leads to death by asphyxiation."

"We're tracing events going back more than eight years since Reginald Pearson's arrest. Over the past five years thousands of people have been victims of St. John's network."

"The victims were promised good paying jobs, modeling contracts, and other higher quality of life opportunities in countries where they didn't speak the language and were unfamiliar with the cultural customs."

"They were threatened and beaten. If they spoke to outsiders, they were told their families would also be punished."

"Many runaway girls got shelter and financial support only to find the payback was prostitution and domestic servitude.

Jon called Richard and asked for two things."

"First, I need you to make some calls to your old military friends who work in high places. I'll be sending them information on St. John's network."

Secondly, assemble a team. I want you to meet that boat in Monaco. I have contacts in Menton, France. They will be very interested in helping you."

Chapter 52

Albany, New York
3:30 p.m.

Darcy Higgins

Darcy Higgins spent the previous night at the Town Place Suites. She spent most of her days wandering the streets. Lonely and afraid, but she knew one thing. She had to come in and talk.

She called the office and was immediately transferred to Ambrosia.

"Did I catch you at a bad time?," she asked in a trembling voice.

Surprised by the call, Ambrosia said, "no I'm sitting here with my brother Richard. We're finishing up the day. We're close to going public and have some important items to finish up before we meet with Chase and the accounting team.

"Are you okay?", I asked. I could feel the tension in her voice.

"I'm ready to come in but I wanted to call you first before I talked with Nathan."

"I think I made a mistake and need to apologize."

"A mistake? Apologize for what?"

"I may be responsible for everything that's happened."

"What are you talking about?"

I put her call on the speaker.

Darcy said, "Gabriel is having financial problems. He owes a lot of money to some dangerous people. I overheard him talking to someone a few weeks ago. He was talking in some kind of code. He said he had some high-priced items that would be good for an auction. The sale would settle his debts. I wasn't sure what he meant but after all that's happened I think you and Vanessa were those items."

I sat stunned, staring at the phone.

Richard saw the strange look on my face.

"Darcy, it's Richard, what's going on?"

She re-summarized her situation.

"I'm scared. I messed up. I don't know what to do."

"Darcy, remember my instructions?"

"Do exactly what I told you to do."

They disconnected.

Richard called Jon.

"Do you know where Darcy Higgins is?"

"Yes, She's somewhere in Albany, New York," he said.

"I've gotta tell you this system these guys have is amazing. I can find anybody, anytime, anywhere. If you have anything electronic or digital on you, I can find and track you."

"What do you need?"

"Is there an FBI office anywhere near her location?"

"Hold on."

"Yeah, there's an office at 200 McCarty Avenue."

"Great, I'll call you later. Thanks!"

Richard dialed Samantha next, asking for a favor.

Meanwhile, Darcy followed Richard's instructions and left her phone in the bathroom of a burger joint. She walked to Lincoln Park and called him with her first burner phone.

"I'm at a park in Albany."

"Go to 200 McCarty Avenue. When you get to the gate let them know who you are. They'll be expecting you. We'll be there in an hour."

"How do I know it's safe?"

"Trust me. When you get there you'll know."

She dumped the phone and started walking.

Twenty minutes later she arrived in front of the Federal Bureau of Investigation building. She went to the entrance and gave them her name.

Thirty minutes later, Nathan, Samantha, Ryan, and Ambrosia arrived.

Chapter 53

Albany, New York
Federal Bureau of Investigation
5:30 p.m.

FBI Office, Albany, New York

Darcy was sitting in an interrogation room when we entered. The reunion was brief.

I embraced her, but felt a detached tension between us.

Our friendship, trust and love had been shattered.

Ryan and I sat in an adjoining observation room to listen to what Darcy had to say.

"Tell us everything. Don't leave anything out," said Nathan.

"I had an affair with Gabriel," she confessed. "I know it's against company policy, but it just happened.

"I know it's against company policy, but it just happened."

"This all started when I noticed some irregularities in our accounts payables. Gabriel was carrying unusually high credit card balances."

"At first, I thought it was a mistake. I didn't know Gabriel had company credit cards."

"I went to Paul asking questions. He said he authorized Gabriel having those cards but would look into the high balances. A week passed and I never heard anything from him. After our last Board meeting, I asked Gabriel if we could talk."

"Did you mention this to Paul or Ambrosia?"

"No, I didn't want to create an issue if there was none."

"Gabriel explained that he was working quietly on investors for our upcoming IPO, but he didn't want to step on any toes. He said his expenditures were legitimate."

"When I approached Paul, he admitted he had approved his expenditures. "I let it go."

"Gabriel started calling me right after that when Ambrosia went on the road. Vanessa was traveling on photo shoots. For weeks I sat home all alone."

"At first he invited me to parties, clubs and then the casinos. I was amazed at who he hung out with. We're talking extraordinarily rich, prominent and well-known people."

"I began to enjoy his company and one thing led to another. I started spending nights with him. A few weeks ago, he started getting phone calls in the middle of the night. A bunch of times he'd get up early talking on the phone. When I questioned him, he said he was working on overseas deals. There were time zone issues."

"A week and a half ago, I knew something was amiss. He was on the phone with someone. He was practically pleading with whoever it was."

"I overheard a conversation about an auction in the French Riviera. He was talking about selling girls. I heard something to the effect that our company had some beautiful women who would bring a nice price."

"I confronted him. We quarreled. His personality changed. He grew vicious. He hit me several times knocking me to the floor. He told me not to stick my nose in his business."

"He said I'd be killed if I breathed a word to anyone. He kicked me out of his apartment. We haven't spoken since."

Something was still off for Nathan,

"You didn't think this was important to Ambrosia or Vanessa?" he asked.

"I know the policy. No fraternizing with the with the office staff or people who do business with the company including board members, contractors and office staff. I knew bringing it up would end my career at CMA. I didn't want to risk that."

Darcy said she had no idea before last weekend that Gabriel had been talking about Ambrosia or Vanessa."

"There's something else few people know about him. He's addicted to gambling. One night he lost $50,000. The next night he won 100,000. He acted like it was nothing."

"To do all the things you said he had to have help. You mentioned Paul. Is there anyone else?" asked Samantha.

"The only other person I know would be Monique. She's just staff but she has way more power and influence than anyone suspects?"

"Nathan and Samantha exited, leaving Darcy along in the room.

Ambrosia was speechless.

Nathan asked her, what do you think about what you just heard?

"It's time for me to clean house." Ambrosia said. "I've got to figure out a way to break all of this to Vanessa and hope she doesn't kill Darcy."

Chapter 54

Manhattan, New York
Federal Bureau of Investigation
8:30 p.m.

Breaking News

The helicopter flight from Albany to Manhattan was somber. Darcy spent the majority of her time weeping. I couldn't stand looking at her. I stared out the window knowing I'd been betrayed.

A million thoughts filled my head. *How could I forgive her? How am I going to spin her confession to Vanessa?*

When we landed, Nathan, Samantha, and Darcy went to the FBI headquarters in New York. Ryan and I went to our apartment, where Vanessa was waiting.

"How did it go?" she asked. "Is Darcy okay?"

I said nothing. Instead, I walked to the window staring at the stars with tears rolling down my cheeks.

"It didn't go as expected," Ryan spoke up.

Stay out of this," I snapped at him.

My breathing got heavy. I paced back and forth in front of the window before turning to Vanessa and encouraging her to sit for what I had to say to her.

I fiddled with my hands nervously rubbing them up and down my sides.

"Give me a minute," I said.

Vanessa sat on the couch. Her heart pounded as she stared bewildered by my behavior.

Ryan took a seat on a kitchen bar stool.

I spoke to her as I looked out the window. Tears flowed as I recounted Darcy's confession.

Vanessa absorbed every word until I finished. She got up and stood next to me and grasped my hand.

"Does she know what happened to me?

"No, no one has told her."

Vanessa pounded the window with her fist. Luckily, her hand didn't go through the glass.

"She betrayed us all." It all makes sense now."

"What! What makes sense?" I asked.

"I've been thinking. Last week when she went for her morning run, she left earlier than usual. She always waits until we were up before she leaves."

"When I heard the commotion in the living room, I came out of my room. That's when I was attacked. The next thing I know I was drugged, handcuffed to a bed and a man was raping me.

235

"You said she didn't know they were coming for us."

"If that's true, why did she leave early that morning?"

Suddenly, Ryan sprang from his seat.

"Wait," he said.

He called Nathan.

"Nathan was in the middle of the interrogation when he saw the caller I.D.

"Is everything okay?

"No, Darcy's not telling you everything."

Nathan headed to the door, giving Samantha the take it from here look.

"What've you got?"

"The morning Vanessa was abducted, Darcy left earlier than usual for her morning run. Vanessa says that was not routine; apparently, she never leaves before they all were up. Why did she leave that part out?"

Nathan stood outside the door seething, his temperature rising.

He reentered the room slamming the door behind him. His action startled everyone.

"Let's go over this again," he instructed Darcy. On the day Vanessa was taken, what happened? Start from the time you woke up."

"I told you; I went for my morning run. When I came back the living room was a mess and Vanessa was gone."

"What time was that exactly?"

"I'm not sure."

He pounded his fist on the table.

"Was Vanessa up when you left?"

Stunned, she said, "I don't know. Why are you asking me that?"

"How's this. You left earlier than usual." You always go running after everyone's up."

"Ambrosia and Vanessa will vouch for that."

"Why did you leave earlier that day?"

Darcy covered her face with her hands, sobbing.

She mumbled, "I screwed up."

Samantha tipped her head, silently motioning for Nathan to step outside. He did, but wanted to know why.

"That call was from Ryan. Vanessa told them Darcy left earlier than usual on the morning of her abduction. She never leaves before they are up. Why did she leave that part out?"

"Good question," she said.

"I need you to step back. Samantha advised. You're mad as hell. You just scared the life out of the poor girl. Let me see what's really happening."

"Wait, you'll know when to come back in."

Darcy looked at Samantha through swollen eyes. She turned nervously from side to side looking for Nathan.

"Tell me what happen the morning of the kidnapping. I want to know everything that happened from the second you woke up until you left to go running."

"You know everything already," she said.

Samantha slapped the table.

"Darcy, we have proof that you didn't tell us everything. Do you want to go home, or shall we arrest you as an accomplice to kidnapping and murder?"

"What! No, wait, wait. What are you talking about?"

"C'mon Darcy. You know what I'm talking about. Answer the question. Was Vanessa up when you left?"

"Okay, okay," she said staring at the floor.

"I got a call that morning. I was told to leave the apartment immediately or else."

"Or else what?" Samantha prompted her,

Nathan re-entered the room.

"Who called?" he asked.

"Paul Gregory," Darcy shared.

"He told me my digging created problems he couldn't fix. If I were there, I'd be a casualty. He hung up before I could ask what was going on, but I remembered Gabriel's threat."

"I was afraid and left as fast as I could. I got back around 9:00 a.m. You know the rest of the story."

"You didn't think to wake Vanessa?

"No, after my melt down with Gabriel, I was afraid to talk to anyone."

Samantha and Nathan left the room.

Samantha asked her partner if he believed they were getting the whole truth. He didn't.

"No, we'll need to probe deeper," he said.

"We already have Paul's phone records. Beyond that we're gonna need some outside help."

"We have that. I'll call Richard," she said.

Nathan came back into the room.

"You said you were looking into accounting irregularities. You talked to Paul. Anyone else?"

Darcy insisted that she hadn't spoken with anybody other than Paul.

"Are you sure?" Nathan pressed.

"Why do you keep asking me this?" Darcy screech while fidgeting in her chair.

"Have you been listening to the news lately?" Nathan raised his voice back at her.

"No, I never turned on the TV or a radio. I ate, slept, and walked. I stayed on the move. After the incident at the apartment, I knew I'd be next.

"Adam Chandler and Helen Grace are dead. Did you know that?"

"What! Oh my God! No, no, no!"

"Come on Darcy, what else do you know?"

She took a deep breath.

"I mentioned it to Helen. I told her in confidence. She's really dead?"

"Yes, she was poisoned the night before Vanessa was taken."

"I swear I only mentioned it to her. I told her I was looking into something. I'd let her know what I found.

"Anything else?"

"She hesitated before auditing that she was the one who posted the missing person's report on both Ambrosia and Vanessa that Saturday afternoon."

"What about Adam Chandler?"

"I don't know anything about him."

"Samantha came into the room and whispered something to Nathan."

"Okay, we're done for the time being," said out loud. to Darcy.

"You're free to go. In fact, we'll take you home," said Nathan.

"Do you think it'll be safe?"

"Yes, we have the building secured."

10:15 p.m.

When they entered the apartment Vanessa greeted Darcy with a smashing right to her face. Ryan quickly intervened before Vanessa could connect with a follow up left. Ryan held Vanessa as she kicked and screamed.

"How could you do this to me while trying to lunge at her so-called friend."

Looking up Darcy, hand on her throbbing cheek repeatedly express how sorry she was."

Vanessa wasn't having it. She struggled to escape Ryan's tight hold until her brother replaced his arms with his own. Nathan whispered something in her ear and her body went limp. Weeping on his shoulder he walked her into her bedroom.

An uneasy silence was broken by a knock at the door.

Edward entered the apartment just as Nathan exited his sister's room.

"We have new assignments," Edward said.

Seeing Darcy laying prone on the floor, he asked what was going on?"

"She tripped and fell," Ambrosia said.

The bruise on her face said something different.

"Yeah, right, said a disbelieving Edward.

He led everyone into Ambrosia's bedroom and closed the door.

"Richard is leaving. He's leading a team to rendezvous with the boat. I'm to stay here with Vanessa as my new assignment."

Nathan was ready to object but was stopped by Samantha. She held up her hand, signaling for Edward to continue explaining.

"The big boss called the office. The call was routed to me. Invisible is doing their own digging into CMA."

"We've got bigger fish to fry," Edward told Samantha.

"We have until Tuesday to wrap this up," Samantha said.

"Tomorrow a lot of heads are going to roll."

"While the FBI will do things by the book, we'll be closing our eyes to Invisible," she said

"This is going to get ugly."

"We'll meet back here at in the morning at nine."

They walked out of the room to find Darcy gone.

Ryan left without comment. He returned eight minutes later, with Darcy.

"I can't stay here," she insisted.

"I messed up. It's best for me to go."

Vanessa wasn't going to let her go a second time.

"We've got too much at stake. Too much to talk about and very little time," she told her friend-turned-foe.

"I'm truly sorry, but terrified. I know it's just a matter of time before Gabrial or one of his associates will find and kill me. I've betrayed everyone. I don't know what else I can do to escape this horrible situation."

"My brother and I had a long talk," said Vanessa.

Nathan told me, "We've all been traumatized by the recent events, especially me. We will never forget what happened to me. But the threat is still real and still out there. We've got to focus on eliminating it by identifying who is behind it before any more damage is done."

"I can't forget the experience but I'll find a way...to maybe forgive you," she said to Darcy.

Tears ran as she spoke.

Ambrosia said, "I understand the feeling. You think you're going to die. God only knows the fear I felt chased by strangers and having to trust and depend on unknown people. I was lost, afraid and would have done anything to escape that situation. But we are together, safe and in one piece."

What can I do to fix this?" Darcy asked.

"Tell us everything you know about Gabriel and Paul," Samantha answered.

"It's more than just them," said Darcy.

Chapter 55

Monday
May 28, 2018
Cosmopolitan Modeling Agency
9:30 a.m.

Chickens Come Home To Roost

Darcy, Samantha, Ryan, and I arrived at the Executive Staff meeting with Jack Puritan.

The meeting had already started. Ryan parked himself outside the front door. Samantha went into Darcy's office.

"Sorry, I'm late," I said. "What'd I miss?"

Jeremy assured me that I didn't miss much, that they were just finishing up the agenda for Friday's board meeting. He asked if everything was okay.

I answered as I continued standing. "No, it's not it but will be soon."

"Where are we?" I asked.

"We have a meeting scheduled with Jack and his accounting staff on Wednesday. I just sent them your report. I'm sending it out to the Board and the underwriters this afternoon," said Jeremy.

Paul handed me the agenda asking, "why Jack was here now?"

Ignoring him I narrowed my eyes on Item 3.

"What is Item #3, Initial Public Offering Redistribution?"

"We're preparing a redistribution of the IPO stocks," said Paul.

"Adam and Helen's death are tragic, but we've got to review our options. Reconsideration of the distribution is one of them."

I nearly lost my balance. I grabbed the side of the table and found an empty chair to sit in.

I thought, *my God, Adam has not been found. Helen's sitting shiva is just ending and we're moving on their shares already!*

"Why is Jack here?" Paul repeated sounding like a broken record.

"Who's preparing this item?" I asked.

"Jeremy and I," responded Paul.

"We've made no decisions, but our thinking is to increase the IPO distribution to the Board and to include the Executive Staff," Jeremy said.

"Our Executive Staff? Whose idea was this?"

"The idea came from me. I've discussed it with the staff. We need to walk through it," said Paul.

"I have a problem with this," said Ambrosia.

"What are you saying?" asked Jeremy.

"The FBI has uncovered evidence of wrongdoing within our firm."

"What are you talking about?" Paul asked, his voice rising.

"Someone cancelled my credit cards and shut down my phone. The calls came from our main telephone number.

"That's ridiculous. I'm the only one with delegated authority to do such a thing?"

"Correction, you, Jeremy and the Board have authority to do that."

I turned to Jeremy, demanding to know if he was aware of Darcy reporting significant accounting irregularities with Gabriel's company credit cards to Paul?"

He denied any knowledge of it.

"Did you know Gabriel beat Darcy and threatened to kill her if she revealed his activities and that Paul knew about it?"

"No, I was not aware of that either. Where are you going with this?"

"Wait a second," Paul intervened.

"I knew Gabriel was working behind the scenes on getting buy-ins for subscriptions to your IPO efforts, but that was all. I had no idea he'd done anything else or that he was making those kinds of a threat."

"Getting subscriptions to the IPO was my assignment and mine alone," said Ambrosia.

"No one authorized Gabriel's involvement. Not Jeremy, myself or the Board."

"That's why Jack is here. I called him this weekend. I want an audit of the accounting records."

"Hold on," Jeremy cautioned. "That requires a closed-door discussion with the Board."

"I know that," said Ambrosia.

"Let me paint you a picture."

"Helen Grace did not die from food poisoning, she was murdered."

"Adam Chandler is missing and presumed dead too."

"Vanessa was kidnapped. By the grace of God, she escaped from being sold in a sex trafficking auction!"

"Multiple attempts have been made to kidnap or kill me!"

"Lucky for us we found Darcy and bought her home. She's confirmed everything I said and is convinced she's going to be next!"

"Now, we have the NYPD and FBI investigating our firm!"

"This has brought us national publicity and a lot of problems we don't need. Unless you want the FBI to invite the IRS in to look into our books, I want Jack to perform the audit before word gets out to the public."

"You all know what would happen if the public found out that the IRS was looking into our accounting practices. The IPO would be dead on arrival."

I looked directly at Paul.

"I've got safeguards in place to protect us now."

"Here's what we're going to do. We're going to table Item 3 and finish the agenda."

"Jeremy and I will handle item three. We'll bring that item to the Board in a closed-door personnel meeting. If anyone has a problem with that speak up now."

"The agenda is fine without item three," said Jeremy.

The room fell silent.

"I guess this meeting is over," said Paul.

"You all know your assignments. We've got lots of work in front of us. Let's get to it," he said.

Everyone left me and Jeremy in the room.

"We're gonna be making some changes around here," I affirmed.

"I didn't want to say it in front of everyone but the FBI is close to finding out who's behind this mess. Arrests are pending."

"Oh, our intimacy policy has been breached too many times. We have to fix that."

"I'm very close to recommending we scrap this whole IPO thing. If we want to raise capital there are alternatives."

"That will require the Board's input and approval," said Jeremy.

"Yes, but with all the press surrounding our firm, I'm not sure our subscription commitments will stand. We can talk to Chase and our attorneys on alternatives. We'll bring that subject up in our closed-door session. Please keep this conversation confidential.

10.40 a.m.

I went to my office. A letter was sitting on my desk addressed to me. It was from Anjelica marked, "PERSONAL AND CONFIDENTIAL"

I read the one-page letter, folded it neatly and put it in my drawer.

I wrote an email to Monica Rodriquez.

Anjelica is leaving the agency. Please readjust the photo shoots with our new model, Sophia.

Ryan and I left for the rest of the afternoon.

Samantha and Darcy left later after giving audit instructions to Jack.

I called Edward from the car.

"Is everything alright there."

"'Vanessa and I are fine. No one told me she could handle firearms as well as any professional."

"There's a lot more to her than that. Did she tell you she's a Gold Awarded Girl Scout and a fifth-degree black belt in Wing Chun?"

"No, but I guess that gives us a lot more to talk about," Edward laughed.

"How goes it with you at the agency?"

"Demand for photo shoots are piling up. We're doing quite well, it seems, despite all of the negative press we're getting." I said before changing the subject.

"Did you get everything?"

"Yep, the recordings came out loud and clear. Everything is set," he assured me.

Chapter 56

Tuesday
May 29, 2018
Monaco
5:30 p.m.

Gabriel

Gabriel laid back relaxing in a lounge chair outside the Monte Carlo Casino. He'd just won $270,000 playing Baccarat. His phone rang while he was admiring a fantastic view of the Mediterranean Sea.

"We've got a problem." The caller said on the other end.

"We've always got problems, he said, irritated. What is it this time?"

"Ambrosia and Darcy came to our executive staff meeting today. They bought our auditor with them. Ambrosia is looking at the books auditing the books. She says there are accounting irregularities involving you."

That got Gabrial's attention.

"I'm listening," he said.

"She pulled the redistribution of the IPO off the Board's open meeting agenda. She's taking it up in their closed-door session."

"Vanessa's brother is an FBI agent. He's investigating our firm. You were named specifically. Paul tried to explain your roll, but Ambrosia killed your credit card authorizations. Ambrosia said the FBI is threatening us with an IRS audit if we don't cooperate. It would kill the IPO if we don't."

The hairs on Gabriel's arm rose. His blood pressure elevated. He sat up straight.

"What do you suggest we do?"

"We! We are not doing anything."

"You do what you've been doing. I'll handle the rest."

Gabrial called Jeremy who demanded to know where the hell he'd been."

"We've been worried that you'd been killed until Ambrosia came in making allegations regarding your involvement in the IPO."

"Calm down, Gabriel hissed. "No one knew this except Paul."

Jeremy wanted to be clued in.

"Ambrosia's work has been great, but she doesn't know I've been working behind the scenes to ensure her marketing subscriptions were successful. I'm out of the country working on a business deal. Email me the Board agenda. I'll call in via a Zoom video conference call for the Board meeting."

Tunis, Tunisia
7:30 p.m.

St John's phone rang. He looked at the caller ID and let it go to voice mail.

Later that evening he listened to Gabriel's voice message.

"St. John, I need an accident in New York. It's time your guys earned their pay. Call me ASAP!"

He didn't call the sniveling man back. He waited until the CMA offices opened the next morning and made a call.

He asked to speak to Jabari Cooper.

"Hi, this is Reginald Pearson. I'm in Tunis, Tunisia. I got a strange call from Gabriel. Can you fill me in on what's going on?"

"I can't talk right now. I'll call you back."

He went into Darcy's empty office.

"Ambrosia came in with a personal bodyguard and the FBI," he shared.

"Our books are going to be audited," he continued. Evidently, Gabriel has been using our agency's account as his own personal bank. Paul's been vague on what he's been doing but Ambrosia is furious and wants the audit. Our plans are going sideways right now."

St. John returned Gabriel's call. The man wanted to know what action he should take and he was informed that there'd been a change in plans.

"That woman is causing me problems I don't need. I want to send everyone a message."

"You know for a guy I've never met you have a way of making demands that don't sit well with me or my people. This is going to cost you."

"Yeah, I know. I'll send you $100,000 in a few minutes. I need this done before Friday."

"You do realize we've got a boat arriving at any moment. I've got an auction to run. I really don't have time for this."

"Look, if the FBI discovers what we're up to it could be trouble for all of us."

"The FBI can be trouble for you. They don't have jurisdiction on me or my operations."

"Well, they can make some calls. Life would be miserable for both of us. Just see what you can do."

"At this late notice I can't promise you anything. I'll tell my boys to be quick. We should meet for breakfast tomorrow."

St. John was tired of Gabrial and didn't like being jerked around. *He's gotta go.*

He made a call to New York. He got no response.

Chapter 57

The Super Yacht

The Espilce, a magnificent 533-foot, $600 million super yacht sailed into Hercules Harbor. It accommodated 36 overnight guests with sleeping quarters for a crew of 70. The 3,600 square foot master suite was comprised of three bedrooms and five full bathrooms. It contains a private great room/kitchen, a full-size private gym, and a wet/dry sauna.

The yacht's individual bedrooms contained remote controlled video cameras and an anti-paparazzi system to shield occupants from unwanted photos.

The yacht had eight decks and two swimming pools. The pool on the upper deck could be covered and converted to a ballroom floor to accommodate live music and several hundred guests for dining, drinking, and dancing. There were also two helicopter pads, a four-person submarine and an anti-ballistic missile defense system on board.

The boat was owned by a consortium and rented out on a regular basis for $15,000 per day.

Twenty-two rooms were marked "Off Limits." Fourteen rooms were reserved for VIP guests who would be boarding over the next 48 hours.

The Monaco Festivities

As was tradition, the infamous Formula 1 Grand Prix de Monaco car race ended in a night of wild partying. Friday opened with the start of the 58th Monte-Carlo Television Festival.

The world renown festival is open to the public and gives fans a once in a lifetime opportunity to mingle with the rich and famous. Fans attended behind the screen conferences and autograph sessions with their favorite actors and actresses.

The Golden Nymphs competition promised to complete the week with red-carpet ambiance and VIP cocktail parties for more than a thousand guests.

Both events provided the perfect cover for St. John's auction. A pilot launch guided the Espilce to its reserved berthing spot in Hercules Harbor.

After more than thirty days at sea the temporary deck crew spent their final hours preparing for time off. Their replacement crew arrived early the next morning.

Wednesday
6:30 a.m.

Riccardo Alessandro arrived for duty with 15-person deckhands. After a two-hour orientation, they were informed the bosun became mysteriously ill. He was rushed to the Centre Hospitalier Princesse Grace. It was uncertain if he'd ever return.

The second officer informed everyone he needed an experienced bosun to lead the arriving deckhands.

Riccardo presented his credentials showing extensive experience. He sat with the Captain, Chief Officer, and deck officers going through the week's itinerary. He was given a special responsibilities list of specific do's and don'ts.

Gabriel arrived just before noon. As a VIP guest, he was given a special room on an upper deck.

St. John appeared around 3:00 p.m. He was given the master suite.

Their first face-to-face meeting occurred at dinner. They exchanged pleasantries and mingled with their special guests. They manage to consult near the end of the evening over caviar and champagne.

Gabriel got right to the point.

"How is it going in New York?"

"It's not. I called my men. I've got nothing. It's not a good sign. She has a highly skilled protective team surrounding her 24/7. She's untouchable."

Gabriel questioned St. John's competence.

St. John's voice trembled, his rage building.

"I've been in this business a long time and I have never, ever failed to deliver. Your people asked me to apprehend several high-end assets, which is not what we do." We've always worked with people on the fringe for a reason. They're less likely to be missed."

"Initially, your request seemed simple. Now, this shit is out of control. It's made the national news for God's sake. I don't need this kind of attention coming down on my business."

"Are you saying the job is beyond your capabilities?" Gabriel asked.

St. John exploded.

"The guys, men I've used for years, are all dead, he raged. How many other have been killed in this? For what, two girls."

Gabrial started to speak, but St John wasn't done. This mess is yours. You clean it up."

"Fine, but I want my $100,000 back," shot Gabriel.

"You can have it," said St. John.

"Done", St. John said as he pulled out his phone and made the transfer.

"Friday night we'll auction off the products. You'll get your 20% cut."

St. John got up and left with a parting comment.

"I know you owe a lot of people. You've made promises you can't keep. My people don't like that."

"You're a pain in the ass and have costs me more than you know."

The conversation was over for St. John.

"When this weekend is done, so are you and I," he said in parting.

Neither men realized the waiter clearing the table was recording their conversation at Richard's behest.

Upon receipt of the intel, a call was made.

"I've got them," Richard said.

"This is going to be easier than I expected," Jon said.

Chapter 58

Thursday
May 31, 2018
New York
10:50 a.m.

The Audit

Jeremy and I sat with Jack Puritan. It hadn't taken long for Jack to find what he was looking for.

For the past two and a half months Gabriel Simon had run up credit card debits of over $650,000.

Jack reports detailed spending at racetracks, casinos, and golf resorts around the world. The largest charges were from the Happy Valley Racecourse, Hong Kong; the MGM Casino in Macau, Aria Casino in Las Vegas, Pine Valley Golf Course, New Jersey, and the Shinnecock Hills Golf Course in Southampton, New York."

"His most recent usage was $50,000 in Monaco. He'd won a lot. He'd lost a lot. Right now, he's $100,000 in debt. The only positive thing I can say is his credit card bills are always paid on time."

Paul Gregory was called into the meeting.

"Did you know about these?" asked Jeremy.

"As I told you before, he was doing business on behalf of the company. I knew he was using his credit cards to conduct business. He'd transfer money into an account we have access too. We'd use that account to keep his bills current. He's never been behind on his monthly payments."

"Hold on" I interrupted.

"I've been gone for five weeks. Jack says he's been doing this for nearly three months. You didn't know what he'd been up to?"

Paul started to speak, but I wasn't finished.

"Gambling is not company business. We are not his personal piggybank. You should have known better," I admonished.

"How many credit cards does he have?" Jeremy asked.

"He has two. A VISA and an American Express."

"Are any other Board members carrying company cards?"

"The executive staff has company cards. They are only used for traveling expenses. We are the only other ones carrying company cards," he said.

"Gabriel is the only Board member with company cards."

"Correction, you two have company cards. Remember mine were cancelled remember?" I added.

"What do you want me to do?" Paul asked.

"Cancel his cards and close his accounts immediately," Jeremy instructed.

"We'll deal with my cards after the Board meeting," I said.

Jeremy nodded his approval.

"We'll put an item on tomorrow's agenda regarding Board members acting on behalf of CMA under new business," I said.

"I agree," said Jeremy.

Jeremy voiced his agreement as Paul and Jack left the room.

"Paul is not telling us everything. His days here are numbered," I said.

"It certainly sounds that way," said Jeremy.

1:00 p.m.

Nathan sat at his desk building a case on specific individuals associated with CMA. The federally approved wire tapes and telephone records they obtained were paying off.

The information he obtained showed incriminating evidence against several CMA staff. Evidence involving the mysterious Reginald Pearson, a.k.a. Raymond St. John to the kidnapping of Vanessa was confirmed. Search warrants were granted, and arrest warrants issued.

"Tomorrow is going to be a big day," Samantha said.

Chapter 59

Friday
June 1, 2018
New York
10:00 a.m.

The CMA Board

The Board meeting started on a conciliatory note but ended badly. The regular business agenda regarding fashion shows, photographic and contractual obligations passed by unanimous consent.

The fireworks started during the closed-door session.

Gabriel attended via video conference call. He raised objections to the postponement of the stock redistribution on the upcoming IPO.

"I am truly saddened by the awful deaths of our fellow Board members, but we need to focus on the future. That future is going public."

He objected to the announcement of the termination of Paul Gregory.

"Whose idea is this? He's done nothing wrong!"

Immediately, I went after him.

"You of all people know exactly what he did wrong," I said.

"You've been manipulating the Board for too long. You helped orchestrate the kidnapping of Vanessa and multiple attempts to abduct me for some sex trafficking scheme."

"You've broken our zero-tolerance policy regarding intimate relations with several staff members," as I continued with a litany of misconduct.

"I don't know what you have on Paul, but it has threatened him enough to get his authorization for you to use our company's assets for your own personal benefit. All under the false assumption of working on our IPO's pre-subscriptions. We have records going back three months to prove it. You and Paul have repeatly lied to us."

Gabriel laughed at me.

"You're suffering from dementia. Have you forgotten we've been talking about the IPO for over a year? Now you're coming in with these delusional accusations!"

"You have no proof."

"I'll be suing you for defamation of character and anything else my legal team will come up with!"

His laughter was more than I could take and I lost it.

"You're a narcissistic sociopath," I yelled at the screen that bought him to the meeting remotely.

"Your sex trafficking boat in Monaco is going down. You'll be arrested and extradited back here for those crimes and as an accomplice in the murder of Adam Chandler and Helen Grace," I shouted.

"You're nothing more than a wanna be con man. You've failed at everything. You'll be locked up or killed before you make it back to the states."

Jeremy slammed his gavel.

"Ambrosia, that's enough," he said, raising his voice.

"These are serious accusations Ambrosia," Juliette spoke up.

"Do you have any proof?"

"Oh, I have plenty of proof." Her question was the perfect segue into me opening the door and inviting FBI agents Nathan Gilbert and Samantha Jackson into the room.

After introductions Nathan didn't mince words.

"At this moment Paul Gregory, Jabari Cooper, Roman Yee, Trina Namibian, and Monique Harding have all been arrested. We've issued a warrant for Gabriel Simon pending his return to U.S. soil. Because this is an on-going investigation, I can't comment on any more than that."

The agents turned and left.

The news sent the room abuzz. Whispers and conversations shot back and forth across the room until Jeremy pounded his gavel over and over again.

"Please everyone, settle down. Let's get back to business."

I motioned for Gabrial's suspension from any further involvement with CMA pending the conclusion of the FBI investigation.

My motion was seconded by Juliette and passed unanimously.

Gabriel ended his virtual participation in the meeting and immediately sought out St. John.

"We need to talk now," he said.

Gabriel recounted what had just transpired during the meeting, purposefully omitting Ambrosia's comment about the yacht being taken down.

St. John didn't like Gabriel and could care less about his problems. He had an auction to complete.

1:00 p.m.

Jeremy and his fellow Board member were stunned, but continued deliberations on other closed-door items.

I was in shock at the mention of Trina's name, but kept my thoughts to myself.

I asked Jeremy for the floor and he slid the gavel to me.

"I am not apologizing for anything I've said."

"You all know I am fully committed to see our organization through whatever happens next."

I pulled a folder from my briefcase and handed out a new agenda and a revised business plan.

"In the coming months we are going to restructure this organization," I announced.

"As we go through this plan, changes will be made but please have an open mind."

"Some of these changes regarding our administrative personnel are going to be painful. We'll employ an executive search firm to fill vacant positions."

The first item on the new agenda was the IPO.

"The Initial Public Offering is going forward. With all the publicity we've endured for the past two weeks and the fact that our business model is exceedingly successful, we have more than enough support to issue the IPO."

"For those of you who don't understand let me make this simple. Our goals have not changed. We will succeed. We will survive."

"In another year we will be the standard of measure in the modeling industry," I assured.

When I was done laying out my vision Claudia motioned approval of the plan, Mario seconded the motion.

The Board gave it unanimous approval and a standing ovation.

Chapter 60

Friday
June 1, 2018
Monaco, France
9:00 p.m.

The Auction

Fourteen VIP guests sat in their rooms listening to their auction instructions on 64-inch television monitors. In the meantime, over 150 guests partied to live music in the ballroom.

Gabriel stood outside looking at the City of Monaco. He kept trying to figure out how things unraveled so fast. He owed over $1.5 million in gambling debts. His options for paying the money back were dwindling.

Earlier that morning the Monaco National Police received an anonymous tip that illicit sexual activities involving minors would take place onboard a super-yacht anchored in Hercules Harbor.

The police mobilized their raiding party at a hotel parking lot across the street.

Gabriel noticed their gathering. A chill ran through him. Ambrosia's threat wasn't an idle one and reality hit him like a bolt of lightning. His blood pressure increased as he ran looking for St. John. He bumped into the captain.

He was out of breath and breathing heavily, but he squeezed out a warning that the police were coming."

"Are you sure?"

"Look!" He pointed to the parking lot.

"They're mobilizing to raid this ship."

The captain cursed.

"Meet me at the submersible and go find St. John," he commanded.

Gabrial found him on the bridge.

"It looks like we're about to be raided!" he said.

"The National Police are coming."

"How do you know this?" St. John demanded.

As he had with the captain, Gabrial pointed to the nearby gathering of law enforcement.

"The captain wants us to meet him at the sub," Gabrial said.

As the gravity of the situation struck him, St. John quickly went to his suite wondering what was happening. He stuffed his overnight bag and met the captain at the elevator.

Gabriel scrambled to his room, grabbed his backpack, got on the elevator, and headed to the aft of the yacht.

Riccardo was dressed in black combat coveralls, standing in the shadows observing Gabriel's frantic behavior. *He's heading downward. His only escape is the submersible.*

Gabriel arrived to find the submarine gone. The bastards left him.

He went back to the elevator where he encountered Riccardo.

"Riccardo the police are coming. I need your help to get out of here."

The man didn't move, despite the urgency of Gabrial's words.

"My name's not Riccardo. It's Richard Alexander," he said, watching as the meaning of his words sunk in."

"Ambrosia Alexander is my sister."

Gabrial was stunned silent and never had a chance to speak. His eyes widened as Richard stabbed him in his spleen.

"That was for Vanessa Gilbert," Richard said before plunging the knife into the man's bladder.

"This is for Darcy Higgins."

Richard slashed Gabrial's throat, dragged his body into the elevator and pushed the button for the ballroom level.

When the door opened a group of guests standing nearby saw his body lying in a pool of blood. Screams echoed across the opulently appointed room. Pandemonium broke out as the police entered guns blazing at armed guards. In the chaos, people ran in every direction.

The auction halted as the police swarmed the lower floors. Gun fire erupted. Several policemen were shot. They returned fire killing three men.

Moving from room to room the police found many women and under-aged girls. All were sedated wearing sexually explicit lingerie.

Richard calmly cleaned himself, his knife and removed his gloves and combat coveralls. Underneath he wore a black tuxedo. He wrapped his combat gear and everything else around a large heavy wrench and dropped them in the water where the mini-sub sat a few minutes ago. He climbed the stairs and merged with the escaping crowd. He met his team in Nice.

He called Samantha.

"We stopped the auction. The women and girls are safe."

"What about our assailants?"

"St. John escaped in a submersible. Gabriel didn't make it. He's no longer a problem."

He called Jon. He already knew.

"I know where St. John is going," said Jon.

"Time to bring down his network."

Chapter 61

Friday
June 1, 2018
Federal Bureau of Investigation
New York
4:30 p.m.

Interrogations

Paul Gregory, Jabari Cooper, Roman Yee, Trina Namibian, and Monique Harding sat silently in separate interrogation rooms.

Nathan and Samantha plotted their interrogation strategy for questioning them.

"I'll work on the women," Samantha said. "You handle the men."

He agreed.

"I'll start with the weakest link, Trina."

<u>Trina Namibian</u>
Samantha smiled as she pulled up a chair close to the women she intended to break.

"Can I get you anything?"

Trina looked at her in total shock.

"Ms. Namibian, do you understand the charges we've bought against you?"

"No. I don't understand any of this." Trina answered.

Samantha moved closer, touching the woman's shoulder.

"Why don't we start with you telling me about yourself?"

"What do you want know?"

"Who is Trina Namibian? You have an African accent, yet I can hear a touch of German. Let's start there."

"My younger sister Petrina and I were born in Namibia. We came here eleven years ago to attend Baruch College. I majored in International Business Relations. She majored in Political Science. We met Jeremy at a business workshop."

Trina described her sister as standing 5'9" tall, possessing a smooth, dark chocolate complexion and a 22-inch waist.

"When Jeremy saw her he couldn't stop staring and drooling all over her," she recalled. She's prettier than I could ever be."

"He asked her if she ever thought about modeling. He invited her to a trial photo shoot and immediately signed her to a modeling contract."

"Ambrosia pulled us under her wing and trained her to become a sensational runway."

"We told her we wanted to stay in the U.S. She agreed and sponsored us. After graduation she offered me a job as an office assistant."

Trina shared her appreciation for Ambrosia's mentorship and ultimate friendship. She spoke of how she worked her way up to a leadership role as Director of Client Services.

"You've being charged as an accessory to the kidnapping of Vanessa Gilbert and the attempted kidnapping of Ambrosia," said Samantha.

"We have phone records that link you to a known sex trafficking criminal who goes by the name of Reginald Pearson. Explain that relationship."

"I don't know the man. We've never met. Paul said he was important. He was supposed to introduce me to some high-profile clients. He'd call all the time asking questions about models. He and his questions made me uncomfortable. I went to Paul about it. He assured me Mr. Pearson was okay. I still had concerns and briefly mentioned it to other staffers."

"A month ago, I got an unusual call from Gabriel. It was out of the blue but he reiterated that Mr. Pearsons was an important confidential client and not to make waves."

"He threatened to have us deported if I caused problems. We only have green cards and visa's. Our applications for U.S. citizenships are pending. Neither one of us has a desire of going back home."

"Paul said Mr. Pearson has a reputation of stealing models from other agencies, but told me to leave it alone. I researched him on the internet, though, and found out he was a sex trafficking fugitive. I tried to talk to Ambrosia, but she was busy getting ready to go on the road. She left before we could talk."

"Two weeks ago, you were in the office. You made a lot of oversees calls. Tell me about them."

"Oh, those calls were with Annika, Lizzie and Moni. Some of their clients were being difficult during the photo shoots. I spent a lot of time that Saturday solving problems. Most of our clients are nice but some are knuckleheads and difficult to deal with."

"Because of them I keep meticulous notes in a journal. You can have them if you want."

"Good, we'll get them later," said Samantha.

"Tell me your feelings about the IPO?"

"I don't have any. I'm happy with everything. I can't speak for the other directors. Some openly grumbled. I don't really care about the IPO. You can't get salaries like this in Africa. I have no issues or complaints."

"How come you didn't tell anyone else about the threats?"

"I don't have a great relationship with the other directors. I think they envy my friendship with Ambrosia. I tried texting her, but she was already on the road. She never got back to me."

"Anything else?"

Trina thought for a moment.

"The only thing I can think of is Monique and Roman. They were in the office that weekend. That was strange."

"How so?"

"She and Jabari were at the front desk. They kept going back and forth from his office for a few hours. I don't know what they were doing. They were very secretive. When I asked them what was going on Monique told me to do my job and mind my own business."

"I have no idea why Roman was in the office."

"Am I going to jail? I didn't do any of that stuff you're charging me with."

"Will I be deported?"

"I don't know what to do."

"Can you help me?"

"I'll see what I can do," said Samantha.

"When can I talk to Ambrosia?" asked Trina.

Samantha went out and conferred with Nathan.

Upon return she informed Trina that she could go home but only after turning over her green card and passport.

"We'll go to the office tomorrow morning. I want that journal."

"Don't speak with anyone about our conversation, not even your sister. Do you understand me?"

"Yes ma'am, I'll do anything you ask."

Monique Harding
Monique sat trembling and fidgeting with her fingers when Samantha walked in.

"Before we get started is there anything I can get you? Water, coffee or a soda?"

She mumbled, "water please."

Samantha sat across the table from her.

"You know we have some serious charges against you," she said.

"Is there anything you'd like to tell me?"

"I was just following orders. Paul assigned me and Jabari to close Ambrosia's credit card accounts and to shut down her cell phone. I have all the authentications and authorizations, but Jabari had the man's voice."

"We used the switchboard to make the calls. No one was supposed to know who made them. He did all the talking. I swear I didn't know Paul was planning to kidnap Ambrosia and all that other stuff. She's been good to me. She's responsible for my promotion. I'd never hurt her."

"I'm curious, what was the motivation behind all of this?" asked Samantha,

"Paul and some of the directors were upset. The IPO is expected to bring millions of dollars to the firm. That's a lot of money. They didn't like being cut out. They agreed on creating a publicity stunt to get us in the headlines as leverage to get us all in."

"Paul gave everyone different assignments. He told each of us not to talk to anyone about who was doing what."

"He said it would protect us if anyone found out what we were up to."

"How does Gabriel fit into all of this?"

"That bastard. He sold the IPO idea to the Board. Ambrosia, Adam, and Helen got into a confrontation with him about it. Jeremy stepped in and stopped the fighting and put it on the agenda. The Board voted in favor of the idea."

"Paul was furious about the whole situation. He thought he should have been included in the earlier distribution. He got Jeremy to promise he would be part of some employee stock option plan. Paul was still grumpy but wanted to keep his job. I didn't know he and Gabriel were working together. I knew they sometimes met but I was excluded from those meetings."

"I never trusted Gabriel. He's smooth and flamboyant. He's always name dropping and bragging about himself. He's the center of his universe."

"How does Vanessa and Darcy play into this?"

"They're original investors."

"As Ambrosia put it—they have skin in the game."

"We all knew they were getting a big piece of the pie.

"A lot of our models are envious of Vanessa. She gets all the attention. Now, she's going to cash out and be rich. It didn't seem fair."

"Darcy is a bitch on wheels. She knows everything that goes on in the agency. She's all about the money and a dictator when it comes to our accounting system. I've watched her bite the heads off of models for submitting flawed payment vouchers. Most of our models hate her.

"Who else knew about this scheme?"

"Nobody, the directors kept their assignments in confidence. I normally sit in on all the meetings. I hear a lot. Paul told me I'm classified as a confidential employee. He laughed and told me on a number of occasions, see no evil, hear no evil, speak no evil. He told me to remember that if I wanted to keep my job."

"You mean Jeremy didn't know?"

"No, Jeremy's too busy kissing the Board's ass."

"Anyway, he has his own little secret."

"What's that?"

"You didn't hear it from me, but he and Anjelica are you know..."

"No, I don't, tell me."

"I'm not sure if Anjelica is faking her affair with Jeremy or if she's for real."

"Her assignment was to watch Jeremy. If he found out anything she was supposed to report it to Paul. I guess one thing led to another. They got serious."

"How do you know all this?"

"Two weeks ago, she spent the entire weekend with Jeremy."

"Did you know that?"

"We know a little bit."

"Do you know why she was there?"

"Enlighten me."

"She was there to make sure he didn't come into the office that weekend. Sometimes he'd come in on Saturdays. If he decided to come that Saturday she was to call me. We were not supposed to be there. We didn't want him seeing us."

"Am I going to jail?"

"I can't answer that. We have a grand jury indictment against you. You will be held until your arraignment on Monday. After your arraignment you may qualify for a pre-trial release."

"You'd better not be lying to me. If I find out you lied to me this will be a different conversation."

Jabari Cooper
Nathan sat across the table.

"Is there anything I can get you?"

"No."

"Mr. Cooper, you've read the grand jury indictments against you and your rights. If you cooperate with our investigation we may be able to offer you some clemency."

He gave Nathan a smug look.

"I didn't do anything."

"Do you know the punishment for aiding and abetting, for being a party to a crime?"

"Kidnapping is a federal offense."

"A conviction gets you 20 years."

Silence.

Nathan called in the U.S. Marshal.

You're going to a Federal Prison facility until your arraignment. That may be some time next week.

"Hold on! I had nothing to do with the kidnapping. I was told to cancel Ambrosia's credit cards and cut off her phone. That's all."

"And…?"

"You already know everything."

"What are you guys offering?"

"Twenty years, maybe a five-year minimum. Refuse to cooperate we'll indict you for everything we can find. Am I making myself understood?"

"Paul's the boss. He gave us individual instructions. I didn't know about the kidnapping. I swear I was in the office working on the Fall marketing calendar. Monique came in for a few hours. She made the calls. I did the talking. That was it."

"Get him out of here," said Nathan.

"Wait! There's more," he said.

"Gabriel is behind all of this. Late one night I heard him and Paul arguing. Paul was always bragging about his mother and some big inheritance, but it's all a lie!"

"His mother was terminally ill and dying. She died a year ago. He never talked about it. During her hospice she was eating money. When she died the trust had to pay for it. It left him penniless. He's an only child. She left him with nothing but bills."

"He filed for bankruptcy a month ago. I saw the paperwork on his desk. He was borrowing money from Gabriel. He tried to conceal that."

"When he found out I knew about it he threatened to fire me if I said anything. I had no idea what he was planning."

The U.S. Marshall took him away.

Roman Yee
Nathan got right in his face.

"You know the charges and your rights. You want to explain anything to contradict what we've got."

"Nope."

"Okay, this'll be quick."

"We talked with your colleagues. They've given you up. Kidnapping is a federal offence. Are you ready to spend the next 20 years in a federal prison?"

"You have an interesting military background. We're digging into your entire career."

His arrogance faded. His body language suggested surrender.

"We're going to talk with your boss."

"You want some water or something while you think on whether you want to talk? Otherwise, this kind Marshall will escort you to your federal accommodations until your arraignment."

"You might be there a while," said Nathan.

Paul Gregory
Nathan sat on the far end of the table staring at him.

After a minute, he asked, "Can I get you anything?"

"My lawyer, Vernon Andretti."

"Sure, call him. You're gonna need him."

"We have your telephone records going back for the past three months. Some of those conversations have some very incriminating evidence. You want to shed some light on those conversations."

"No."

"By the way, Gabriel can't help you. He was caught on a yacht in Southern France. We've collected his telephone and computer. A warrant to search his apartment is being executed as we speak."

"We have evidence on you, him and that military group in California."

"In addition to the kidnapping and attempted kidnapping charges, we're charging you with participating in a sex trafficking network and orchestrating the murder of Adam Chandler and Helen Grace."

"You're looking at 25 years to life and maybe the federal death penalty."

"We know you're in debt and filed for bankruptcy. Care to comment on that?"

He sat stoic, staring at the ceiling.

"Just so you know we have a warrant to search your premises as well."

"I am curious about one thing. Was money the only motivation here?"

His eyes glassed over. Wrinkles appeared across his forehead.

"I had nothing to do with any killings," he said. "I want my lawyer."

"Officer, please take him into custody."

Chapter 62

May 28 – June 1, 2018
Lafayette, CA

The Network

During the week anonymous tips flooded in from around the world, shutting down St. John's human trafficking network. It started with information arriving at the U. S. Department of Justice, the State Department, and the Defense Intelligence Agency.

Over that same seven-day period Slim hacked into nearly all of St. John's bank accounts. He became St. John. He changed all of his passwords, dual authentication system questions and answers.

He and Jim slowly liquidated all of St. John's funds. They were electronically transferred to ISC's offshore accounts. For banks where they could not break into, information found its way to other international government agencies who froze those accounts.

Accounting information on his money laundering activities and the location of his financial institutions arrived at the office of the U.S. Internal Revenue Service.

The FBI and the NSA led raids that covered more than 70 cities. They found many children from orphanages and foster care homes victims of the sex trafficking.

Evidence arrived at the desks of the attorney general's office in the states of Ohio, Missouri, Texas, Michigan, and California exposing sex trafficking operations that ran through escort services and massage parlors.

Police officials from Washington D.C., Chicago and Arizona were arrested for protecting pimps and prostitution rings. An officer in Arizona committed suicide shortly after his arrest.

Authorities world-wide arrested more than 500 people including high ranking law enforcement personnel, judges, elected officials, wealthy businesspeople, and well-known celebrities.

Information secretly found its way to government authorities in the Philippines, Pakistan, Thailand, China, India, and Bangladesh.

In the tiny Republic of Montenegro police raided a sex trafficking hotspot and found an embarrassing situation—the operator was the country's Deputy State Prosecutor. He was arrested along with other government officials who ran prostitution operations through Moldavia, Ukraine, and Romania.

Sixty sex trafficking organizations worldwide received information on St. John's human traffickers including the DeliverFund.com, an intelligence website organized to combat sex trafficking. They initiated cyber-attacks on his auctions and worked with many local law enforcement agencies in taking down major portions of his network.

Undercover operatives from the CIA, NSA, and the Internal Affairs Divisions of law enforcement agencies from New York across the United States to Los Angeles raided many of his human trafficking and prostitution shops.

Information poured into the National Human Trafficking Hotline. The hotline helped take down one of the largest human trafficking networks in the United States.

Chapter 63

Saturday
June 2, 2018
Gaua, Vanuatu Islands
7:30 p.m.

On The Run

St. John flew directly from Tunis to Gaua, a small island in the South Pacific Ocean north of the Republic of Vanuatu.

Sweating profusely, he felt the price of failure weighing in on him. This was his biggest failure. Countless clients had been apprehended in the raid on the yacht. The few who escaped were not pleased with the close call. Retribution would be swift.

The next morning, he caught the international news. The French authorities and the Monaco National Police raided the super yacht in Hercules Harbor exposing the sex trafficking auction. There were arrest warrants issued for him, the captain and other people listed on the ship's manifest.

St. John now ranked as one of the worlds most wanted fugitives. Both of his names went viral , as did his before and after surgery photos.

Vanuatu wasn't an extradition country. That bought him a little time. He went online to pay for the yacht rental. His debit card was declined. He knew he had over $5 million in that account.

He spent hours going through his many accounts. All of his passwords failed. After three attempts he was locked out of those accounts.

Trying to figure out what was going on, he dialed a bank in the Cayman Islands only to discover his cell phone did not work.

Using his land line, he called his cell phone. He received a familiar message— *the number you dialed is no longer a working number.*

He called the international bank manager at Credit Suisse in Switzerland. Before the bank representative could provide any information he had to go through their security protocol authentication process.

He couldn't answer any of his security questions and was told if he suspected any fraudulent activity with his accounts, he'd have to come in with the appropriate identification. They couldn't investigate anything until then.

He called CMA.

The receptionist transferred his call to Ambrosia.

He didn't recognize my voice, "My name is Reginald Pearson. I'm calling for Monique Harding."

"She's not available, can I take a message."

"I spoke with her last Friday about an appointment with Trina Namibian. I was calling to confirm our appointment."

She put him on the speaker phone while making small talk about the details of his upcoming appointment.

Ryan interrupted.

"Reginald Pearson, Raymond St. John or whoever you are, this is Rhino. I regret to inform you Monique is no longer employed here. She's in the custody of the Federal Bureau of Investigation."

"She's singing like a canary."

"I know where you are. I'm coming for you."

St. John quickly hung up.

Ryan called Jon.

"I hope you finished the trace on his call?"

Jon answered laughing.

"Yes, he's in the Vanuatu Islands."

In the background you could hear Slim laughing too.

"Now that I've got his land line number he can't go anywhere in the world without me knowing it, said Slim."

"His world is collapsing. This leaves him with one option," said Jon.

"He'll need to disappear."

"What do you want me to do?" asked Ryan.

"Help him."

Chapter 64

June 2, 2018
New York
10:30 a.m.

The Truth

The group gathered at our apartment.

Richard gave a storybook version of what happened on the yacht.

Nathan explained as much as he was allowed to on the grand jury indictments and subsequent arrests.

"I can't believe Trina's involved in this," Ambrosia said.

"I sponsored her and Petrina."

"Are you sure she's involved?"

"Honestly, I don't think she is," said Samantha.

"She turned her journal over to me this morning. She has a lot of overseas calls in the past month. She claimed they were business calls."

"We're matching up the journal data with her phone records. She may be guilty of being in the wrong place at the wrong time. I'll know by tomorrow. We let her go but took her green card and passport.

"Monique is another story. She claims she was following orders, but her telephone records say something different.

Darcy jumped in.

"Don't believe a word she says."

"Why is that?" asked Samantha.

"She's promiscuous. She's slept with Gabriel, Paul, and many of the photographers and agents that come through our agency."

"She manages all of our in-house staff. She knows everything about everybody. She is very good at managing and organizing but she has a dark side few know about."

"How do you know all of this?" asked Nathan.

Darcy's head dropped, her eyes staring at the floor.

Vanessa answered for her.

"You know because you've been chummy, chummy with her from the get-go. Stop with the lying! It's time you told us the truth."

Darcy spoke through falling tears.

"Adam's death was no accident. He was killed by some military guys. When he didn't like the idea of the IPO, Gabriel tried to persuade him. He wined and dined him. He even tried to bribe him for his cooperation. That was an insult and he let Gabriel know it."

"I have to take some responsibility for Helen's death. I told her what Gabriel was up to. She told Adam.

"After the blowup with Gabriel, Adam encouraged her to blow the whistle."

"I overheard Gabriel talking on the phone. They were talking about poisoning someone in New York. I didn't know he was talking about Helen."

Ambrosia stood and shouted, "take some responsibility!"

"For God's sake Darcy. Are you serious!"

"What is wrong with you?"

"Have you lost your mind?"

"We're roommates and business partners."

"We trusted you."

Vanessa leaped off the couch. Edward stepped in front of her.

"Not here, not now," he whispered.

She pushed him off, stomped into her room and slammed the door. He followed her.

He came out a few minutes later.

Nathan asked, "how is she?"

"She's broken hearted and very angry."

"What did you tell her?"

"Let's talk about that later."

"Go on Darcy, what else is there?" asked Nathan.

"Ambrosia is right about Trina. She's innocent, but timid and very naïve."

"The executive team knew her weakness. They used it at every opportunity to manipulate her. She's insecure and does what she's told."

Ryan listened but kept an eye on me. I was moving and pacing again. This time my stride was different.

He followed me into the kitchen. I pulled a butcher knife from its block and turned towards Darcy.

With everyone focused on her, he cut me off and casually took my hand.

"Save this for another time," he said.

He quietly placed the knife back into its place. I fell onto his shoulder. You could hear the muffled sound of me weeping.

"We need a break," he said.

"Let's go for a walk."

I didn't argue and headed towards the door. As I passed Darcy, I backhanded her across her face. Ryan pulled me out the door screaming."

"I confided in you! You knew all along there was a conspiracy and you said nothing!"

We got on the elevator, my tears streaming upon his shoulder.

I sobbed, "who can I trust?"

"You can trust me," he said.

He pulled me closer to him. I didn't resist. We walked five blocks to Central Park.

"Thank you," I said.

"I was ready to kill her."

"Just doing my job."

I continued to vent about this whole ordeal as we walked. He was quiet, just listening when my eyes focused on his.

His look was unusual.

"What's the matter?" I asked.

"I have a couple of things to tell you."

"I have to leave."

"We're tracking St. John."

"He made a mistake and called a bank in the Cayman Islands."

"Apparently, he has a safe deposit box no one knows about. He made an appointment for Wednesday. I'm going to take care of him. Once we're done with him you'll be free."

"Where does that leave us?" I asked.

"With St. John and the others eliminated you won't need a bodyguard anymore."

"That's not what I meant."

"Where does that leave us?"

"Yeah, That's the second thing," he said.

"I've been asking myself that same question. I wasn't supposed to, but I've gotten attached to you. I like you a lot. Being with you is like walking in fresh air. I don't want to leave but I don't really care for New York. I work out of Los Angeles."

I squeezed his hand.

"I've gotten attached to you too."

"What are we going to do?" he asked.

We sat on a bench across from the Hallett Nature Sanctuary holding hands in silence pondering the question.

"I've lived in New York since college, but I realized how much I miss my family."

I put my hands on his face and gently kissed him.

He responded.

The kiss deepened. An elderly couple passed by and I overheard the man tell his companion, "they should get a room."

"I remember something you said."

"Yeah, what was that?"

"Wherever she goes, I go."

Our eyes never wavered from each other.

"Where you go I'm going."

"I'm not sure how I'm going to do it, but I want to be with you if that's okay."

The grin on his face said everything.

We got up and headed back to the apartment.

"Oh, one more thing," I said.

"What's that?"

"No more sleeping on the couch."

For the first time he couldn't stop smiling.

Ninety minutes later we arrived to flashing red, blue, amber, and white lights. A fire truck, an ambulance and two NYPD patrol cars were parked out front. The crowd separated when the gurney came down.

Everyone from the apartment followed.

"What happened?" I asked.

"Darcy tried to commit suicide," said Samantha.

"Right after you left she took some tea into her room. We thought she went to sleep. After about forty minutes I knocked on her door. It was locked. She wouldn't answer. I kicked in the door and found empty bottles of Nyquil and Benadryl on her dresser. She drank the whole bottle and took the entire supersized bottle of maybe 48 pills."

"She left two notes and a signed confession. A note for you and one for Vanessa. We have her confession. It contains information that the FBI is investigating. The notes are upstairs. I'm going with her. Nathan can tell you everything else."

Samantha climbed into the ambulance.

Trina and Petrina watched from the crowd. The sisters were following a group into the lobby when I spotted them.

We ran to each other. Trina wept as she hugged me. Petrina tried to console her as we all embraced.

"She didn't do anything wrong," said Petrina.

"I know, I know," I said.

"Let's go upstairs."

"No, no you don't know. There's more," she said.

A million questions ran through my head. What more could there be?

Chapter 65

Monday
June 4, 2018
New York
8:30 a.m.

The Arraignment

Paul Gregory, Jabari Cooper, Roman Yee, and Monique Harding stood in the federal criminal court before the Magistrate, Judge MaryAnn Lee. I sat with Vanessa, Trina, Richard, Edward, and Petrina. We sat in the audience behind the prosecution amongst a vast media audience.

All of the defendants held copies of the indictments against them which were also read aloud.

The judge asked if they understand the charges against them and their rights. Each affirmed they did. They were then asked how they wanted to plea.

Roman's attorney, Walter Schoch, Jabari's attorney, Adriane Piece, and Paul Gregory's attorney Vernon Andretti all entered not guilty pleas for their clients. Each asked the Magistrate for separate trials and to be released on their own recognizance.

Monique's attorney Ronald J. Smith stated, "my client has pertinent information that may exonerate her from most of these charges."

"She pleads not guilty to the charges of aiding and abetting in the murders and participating in the sex trafficking charges."

"She pleads guilty to being an unwitting participant in the kidnapping charges. In return for her testimony against the other defendants she'd like to be released on her own recognizance."

An objection came from April May, the United States Assistant Attorney for the Southern District of New York.

"The government is requesting all the defendants be held without bail. The FBI has substantial evidence in this case. Telephone recordings and call transcripts point to their involvement."

"They show Ms. Harding in particular, supplied Mr. Gabriel Simon with information about the decedents' schedules. He in turn communicated this information to a Mr. Raymond St. John who had his military operatives orchestrated carry out the murders."

"International and domestic arrest warrants have been issued for Mr. St. John in France and Monaco. He's being charged as an accessory to two murders, a host of kidnappings and operating an international human trafficking network. He is also a wanted fugitive in the United States under the RICO Act."

"Instructions were given to him by Mr. Simon to eliminate Adam Chandler and Helen Grace. The FBI has identified the poison used to kill Helen Grace and the persons who instituted the crime. All of our information points to one clear motive—financial gain. The charges are all in the grand jury indictment. Details of these charges will be shared during the discovery phase of their hearings."

"Have the perpetrators of these alleged crimes been apprehended?" asked Judge Lee.

"No, your honor," stated attorney May.

"Many of the assailants have been killed in confrontations with local law enforcement in California, Nassau, Bahama and on the French Riviera. It is there where Mr. Simon's body was found on a yacht. We have requested a copy of his autopsy from the Monaco authorities to confirm the exact cause of his death."

"Let me see if I understand this. You have not apprehended any of the perpetrators?"

"The FBI has not apprehended the others but received information from an anonymous source that they are no longer a threat," replied attorney May.

The magistrate frowned.

"This court is adjourned until 4:00 p.m. Counselors see me in my chambers, now!"

Once they filed out of the courtroom, the judge voice her confusion.

"After reading the charges everyone seems to be an accessory to crimes committed by perpetrators who are either deceased or on the run. Now you want me to hold them indefinitely based on circumstantial evidence? "What is really going on with this case?" she asked.

Of the four attorneys, it was May who spoke first.

"It's complicated. We are having jurisdictional challenges obtaining verifiable information from international, local law enforcement agencies and a private security company," said attorney May.

"The FBI has identified an organization of ex-military men. They are mercenaries and assassins for hire. They operate a worldwide deep cover human trafficking network."

"The FBI is diligently working on closing the case against them."

"As I stated in the grand jury indictment, we have solid evidence that the individuals arrested were direct participants in all of their charges."

Attorney Andretti jumped in.

"This is a charade."

"The prosecution can't come up with a single eyewitness to prove my clients participation in these crimes."

"My client has lost his job. His reputation is smeared. He wants to be released to clear his name."

"He's innocent of these charges. We'd like our opportunity to prove his case in court."

Each of the attorneys made similar statements with the exception of Monique's.

"Everything that has been said is not factual," said attorney Smith.

"My client has compelling exculpatory evidence and is willing to testify against the defendants."

"Are you plea bargaining counselor?" asked Judge Lee.

"Yes your honor. We are prepared to do just that. I would like to request some time with the prosecution to consider what she has to offer."

Andretti rose from his chair.

"I'll see you in court counselor."

As the other attorneys hurried to leave attorney May stated, "in cases like these we may not win on every count, but we have a duty to see that justice is served for the victims who have lost their lives."

"We have a strong case backed by solid evidence that shows these defendants knowingly participated in the crimes they've been indicted on, otherwise I would not be here."

When they were gone, attorney May spoke directly to the magistrate.

"Your honor there are some things that I could not discuss in front of the defense."

"Explain yourself and this had better be good," she warned.

"The FBI caught one of the perpetrators. His jaw was broken by one of the victims. It is difficult for him to talk. Officers from the private security firm also captured another assailant. He's been turned over to the FBI. He revealed the leaders of this organization, their motives and their base of operations."

"Their facility was raided by the security firm, which to my understanding ended in a fierce gun battle. In that raid the leaders disappeared. Several survivors flipped. We have granted them immunity for their cooperation and information."

"They've given us access to a sophisticated information technology system that exposes a worldwide sex trafficking network. Their system contains voice recordings on murders and money laundering activities in domestic and international banking companies."

"In total the FBI is closing down a $250 million human trafficking network."

"We have evidence of a mole operating inside this group of defendants. The FBI is close to identifying this individual and bringing them to justice."

"Why are you telling me this now?"

"The modeling agency is a legitimate business with world-wide clientele. Several of the victims are employed by the firm. They will be presented as witnesses to testify to the crimes of these individuals which includes our mole."

"Somehow the mole has been using the firm as a front to vet single women entering a human trafficking network."

"From the information we've received thus far we have identified many very high-profile political individuals. These are super rich and powerful people. They employ mercenaries who will kill anyone who can expose their secret activities. You and I are included on that list."

"We had three victims."

"The third victim committed suicide."

"She left a handwritten confession which was obtained by the FBI. It described her involvement and the threat of being killed if she talked."

"In her dying signed confession, she identified several of the defendants. She concluded her confession saying she would rather die by her own hands rather than be murdered by one of their assassins."

"Now that charges have been made public, we've created a life and death situation for all of us."

"The remaining two victims are under 24-hour protection because the threat to them is still active."

"The prosecution would like to remain silent on this information until the discovery hearing before we share it publicly."

"I am not sure I like this. With this information you're making my decisions difficult," said Judge Lee.

"I apologize but we need to protect the victims especially you, I and other innocent bystanders."

4:00 p.m.

"Judge Lee opened the hearing by stating that all of the evidence presented thus far is circumstantial.

With no individuals who actually committed these alleged crimes in custody, I am having difficulty holding these people indefinitely."

"Yet considering the seriousness of the charges, I am authorizing the release of the defendants Paul Gregory, Roman Yee and Jabari Cooper pending receipt of a $500,000 bond and submission of their passports."

"None of you are allowed to leave the city limits for the duration of your proceedings. Court will reconvene here at 8:30 a.m. tomorrow."

The three men posted a 10% bond and were released that night.

Monica Harding was released on a bail of $100,000 the next morning after the prosecution and the defense agreed on her exchange of evidence against the other defendants.

Chapter 66

Wednesday
June 6, 2018
The Cayman Islands
11:30 a.m.

The Last Flight

Raymond St. John entered the British Trade and Commerce
Bank in the Cayman Islands. He disguised himself as before.
He was unshaven and dressed in khaki colored cargo pants,
a blue and yellow flowery island shirt wearing white deck
shoes, with no socks. His flowing blond hair sat neatly under
a wide-brim straw hat. His contact lenses made his coal-
colored eyes blue.

He presented his passport and a U.S. Driver's License
under the name Ronald Jefferson. He strolled out of the bank
thirty minutes later with $300,000 stuffed in a duffle bag.

He stopped at a local café across the street from the
bank to get a bite to eat before boarding a private jet to
Venezuela. He sat at a table in the back near an exit facing
the front door. He ordered a jerk chicken sandwich and an
ice-cold Tazo passion tea.

A group of men came in and sat at the bar. They
talked loudly while watching a soccer game and laughing
with the bartender.

Upon receiving his meal, he reminded the waiter that
he'd also ordered an iced tea. It was bought to him shortly
thereafter.

St. John watched the men as he ate. They were having animated conversations about the game.

He looked around for the waiter to pay his bill. No one was there.

St. John tried to stand and found the task difficult. Anxiety struck him and he felt a tremendous urge to fall asleep. He sat back down in his chair.

Simultaneously he found his vision impaired. He was still able to see a large, muscular man walking towards him from the bar.

"I told you I was coming for you," the man said.

St. John woke up to find himself flying in a small six-seater turboprop, single engine airplane. He looked around lightheaded. There were no pilot in the cockpit. No flight attendant. The back door of the plane was flapping open.

Frantically he tried to lay his eyes on his duffle bag. It was nowhere to be seen. He searched his pockets. Nothing. From the window to his left, he could see the Atlantic Ocean.

He struggled his way to the cockpit and took a seat. He desperately fought the drugs clouding his head. He was trying to understand the flight instrument panel when he saw the plane was locked in autopilot mode. He fiddled with the radio, praying he'd find someone to help him. He noticed he was flying at an altitude of 20,000 feet.

Suddenly, the engine sputtered. Smoke filled the cabin. The engine cut out completely and he felt the plane nosedive. A blinking red light and a loud beeping sound demanded his attention. Both sounds were emanating from a timer placed under the co-pilot's seat.

Time was up. The plane exploded and crashed into the ocean.

Chapter 67

June 13, 2018
8:30 a.m.

Discovery

Attorney May opened her case against each of the defendants starting with Paul Gregory. She laid out how he skillfully arranged and executed a publicity stunt to bring attention to the CMA.

During her remarks, his bankruptcy situation, and the deal he made with Gabriel came to light as well as his lies to Jeremy and Monique

She repeated an earlier statement made by Paul where he swore he had nothing to do with the murder of Adam Chandler or Helen Grace.

She said, "he told everyone how surprised he was to hear about the kidnapping of Vanessa and the attempted kidnapping of Ambrosia. He claimed entrapment, saying he only agreed to play along to protect his job and reputation.

Attorney May continued, "after Paul heard a recording of his phone call to Darcy, it put him in direct contradiction with his claim of innocence. He then admitted that he was aware of what was happening but said he would have been killed if he did not cooperate.

The prosecutor closed her case against him with greed being his main motive.

With the indictment, accessory to murder charges were added to the aiding and abetting in both kidnapping attempts. Paul's bail was revoked and he was immediately taken into custody.

Attorney May stated, "Jabari Cooper lied about his innocence. Voice recordings clearly pointed to his involvement."

As a result, his charges were reduced to aiding and abetting in attempted kidnapping and fraudulently closing down Ambrosia's credit card accounts and cell phone. He would remain free on bail until his trial began.

The bombshell came when May provided a copy of the deposition from Monique Harding and a signed confession from Darcy Higgins.

In that confession, Darcy wrote how she and Monique had been recording all of the agency's phone calls since the company's inception. The recordings were backed up on a redundant server and stored off-site. Very few people knew about them.

Monique collected the recordings and swapped out a new drive every quarter. She turned the audio over to the FBI as part of her plea agreement.

The recordings captured conversations between Roman and two of his old army buddies, Sergeant Major William Berryman and Corporal Stone Phillips. Those recordings were linked to the Exterminators, a group of for-hire mercenaries who worked for the Elegant Modeling Academy out of Florida.

Sgt. Berryman was heard describing how Adam Chandler was going to be disposed of-a month before it happened.

In his final statement he said, "they may never find him. If they do it will be years from now when the river runs low."

The FBI combed the riverbed for miles downstream. They found Adam's body. It matched his description. His waders were filled with rocks which held him down in forty feet of water.

Berryman could be heard telling Roman, "Helen Grace would be eliminated by one of their best men who had taken a job posing as a waiter at her favorite restaurant. She was scheduled to have dinner there with her pregnant daughter."

"No one will know what hit her," he said cavalierly.

On the morning of Vanessa's abduction, Roman went into the office to monitor her kidnapping and to ensure Ambrosia fell into the arms of Raymond St. John. The FBI matched his voice recording to the phone records of calls he made to California.

Roman didn't count on Ambrosia having help. His plan fell apart when Vanessa escaped and both women showed up at the office.

His indictment was upgraded to murder and kidnapping. He too was taken into custody with his bail revoked.

317

The FBI had its hands full, going through years of phone messages, but attorney May was optimistic about them all being reviewed before the men's trials began.

Chapter 68

July 4, 2018
6:30 a.m.

Loose Ends

Three weeks later, separate trials for Paul Gregory and Roman Yee were scheduled. Their trials would begin Monday, July 9, and July 11. Jabari Cooper's trial was scheduled to start the following week.

On the 4th of July, a delivery van marked Fresh Foods drove into the parking garage of the apartment complex at 242 West 53rd Street.

"I have a delivery of fresh vegetables and flowers. They are for Ambrosia Alexander and Vanessa Gilbert, Unit 63A," said the driver.

The guard opened the electronic gate to the garage. The driver pulled a cart carrying a large cardboard box marked perishables and a large bouquet of day lilies and roses to the front desk.

The guard reached for a visitor's form. When he looked up he was staring down the barrel of a small caliber pistol with a suppressor attached. The delivery driver motioned the security guard into the elevator. Once they stepped in, he push the button and headed to the second floor communications center.

The man shoved the guard into the room and promptly shot him in the back of the head. A few feet away a woman sat speaking into a phone. Before she turned to face him, he shot her twice. He moved with purpose, turning off all the video feeds throughout the complex. He pocketed the recorded disks from the computers, put on a ski mask and headed back to the elevator.

With the keys he'd taken off the security guard, he quietly entered Ambrosia's apartment. He grabbed a pillow from the couch and walked down the hallway towards the bedrooms. He opened a door and stepped into darkness. Using the pillow to muffle the sound of his gun, he put two bullets in the back of a blond head. He quickly walked to an adjoining bedroom only to find it empty. Stepping into a third dark bedroom, he put two slugs in the red-haired sleeper.

He was walking back through a nearly pitch-black living room when he felt movement behind him and spun around.

A powerful blow knocked him out.

When he regained consciousness, he was in the same room, tied to chair. His ski mask was yanked off and a 150-watt bulb was shoved into his face. The bright light was blinding and burned his skin.

FBI special agents Gilbert and Jackson were standing in front of him. Ryan Norris and the Alexander brothers sat on bar stools on each side of him.

"Jabari Cooper. You almost got away with it," said Nathan.

"We talked with my father," said Richard.

320

"He knew everything about the financials of every person in the agency."

"You've had a lot of investment transactions over the past four and a half years. His tip led us back to the beginning of the formation of the agency. We've reviewed every telephone conversation."

"We finally finished our review of all the old telephone recordings Monique provided us. At first we couldn't figure it out. Than we heard recordings of you talking with Reginald Pearson more than four years ago," said Nathan.

"The more we listened the more we learned."

"You've been the mastermind behind this whole operation from day one."

"You were hired for your marketing expertise, but in real life you were working deep cover with Mr. Pearson. Your goal was to identify, vet and recruit innocent girls and boys into his sex trafficking network," said Samantha.

"Roman's hire became a plus for your work. His position as the director of human relations and his connections with his old army buddies gave both of you the perfect cover for your operation."

"You convinced Roman to create an employee relations and development manual. He aligned his program to fit your marketing program. The two of you conspired to send women, boys and girls who didn't make the initial modeling auditions to the Elegant Modeling Academy in Florida under the false pretense of training." said Samantha.

"No one suspected the connection between CMA and the Elegant Modeling Academy. Everyone thought it was a copycat of the John Roberts Power's Modeling School."

"During your arrest we got a warrant to search your apartment. We found your files hidden in the floor of your closet," Nathan shared.

"We made copies of everything and left it as we found it. You never knew we were there," Richard said.

It was your meticulous records that helped us piece together the entire scheme, Nathan felt compelled to thank Jabari, the words dripping with facetiousness.

"Roman kept files too," Eddie added. "His revealed how he used his program to vet everyone to ensure they had little, if any, family ties. The Exterminators did the dirty work. Both of you knew these people wouldn't get much attention beyond a few missing person's reports by concerned family or friends. Those reports went nowhere."

"When Reginald Pearson got arrested, jumped bail and ran, that screwed up your cash flow. It took him a while to get back into the business," said Nathan.

When he did, both of you used Gabriel's inflated ego to suggest CMA take the company public. It was a real shot at millions. Everything went well until the staff got cut out of the deal," said Richard.

"The Exterminators were very good until they came after my sister," said Richard.

"After that you all got sloppy. You never knew the system Monique and Darcy created recorded all office numbers, including company cell phone records. We have recordings of every conversation," said Nathan.

"We have voice prints too."

"Once Roman heard the recordings he filled in the blanks. He's been talking a lot to save himself from the death penalty."

Samantha read the charges against him.

"You're under arrest on four counts of murder, two counts of attempted murder, kidnapping and being a member of a major sex trafficking network."

Nathan read him his Miranda Rights.

"What do you have to say for yourself?" asked Samantha.

Before he answered, Vanessa and I walked through the front door of our unit.

His face registered his shock at seeing the women. He had just put bullets in their heads. How were they here now—breathing and unbloodied? As everyone else in the room wore conspiratorial smiles, Jabari grew noticeably pale.

"How does it feel to think you extracted revenge only to find a tighter noose around your neck?" said Ryan.

"The ladies are very much alive and will testify against you in court," said Samantha.

"We set up our own independent camera system. It's been running since Ambrosia and Vanessa returned. You were seen a couple of times scouting the building," said Richard.

"We knew you were coming. It was just a matter of time," he said.

"You didn't know security was on the phone warning us when you entered the elevator. You killed two innocent people."

"For what? What a waste of lives," said Nathan.

"Yeah, we just didn't know when until you drove up," said Edward.

"We moved the ladies to another apartment. You shot two mannequins."

"You're going to prison for a very long time. You qualify for the death penalty too," said Samantha.

"I want my lawyer," Jabari said.

Richard stood, "you won't need a lawyer."

Nathan stopped him.

"Nope, I can't let you do that here. I would love for you to do that, but..." he winked.

Ryan broke his jaw, knocking him out. Handcuffed, he was taken into custody.

The next morning, charges for operating a human trafficking organization under the RICO Act were added to an burgeoning list of offenses, as were two additional counts of first degree murder, two accounts of attempted murder, one count of kidnapping and an attempted kidnapping.

July 17, 2018
12:30 p.m.

Jabari was shackled, handcuffed to his waist and his legs. He shuffled to his trial from the NYC Metropolitan Correctional Center behind the Thurgood Marshall, United States Courthouse in Foley Square, New York.

The square was packed with people buzzing with the frenzied noise of life in the Big Apple.

Jabari stumbled and fell to the ground. When the officers accompanying him got him to his feet, they saw blood spreading from a single gunshot wound in the upper middle of his chest. No one heard the shot or saw where it came from. The officers scrambled in vain to locate a shooter. An ambulance arrived, but their ward was already dead.

Chapter 69

October 5, 2018
The NASDAQ
New York
12:00 noon

The IPO

Three months later, Katherine Weinstein, our new CEO implemented an aggressive marketing and public relations campaign. Katherine filled the company's vacancies with colleagues brought over from her previous firm.

Jack Puritan joined the team as director of finance and accounting. Juliette Jones became the full-time chief legal counsel, reducing her time at Columbia University to adjunct professor. The company went public the first Thursday in October. The offering was issued one hour before the market closed.

Friday morning started slowly. Near the close of business Eastern Standard Time, the stock roared past its initial public offering of $3.75 to $5.63 per share. Over $40 million in capital was raised net of fees.

The CMA split into two offices.

Jeremy remained Chairman of CMA, Board of Directors, New York. His love affair with Anjelica became strained after he found out what she had done. That disappeared once he realized she had been manipulated and how much he really loved her. They married.

Jeremy continued to promote the supermodel class in the high fashion, photography, and film genre worldwide.

I maintained my position as Co-Chair of the CMA Board. I relocated to Southern California opening the Cosmopolitan Modeling and Training Academy of Los Angeles.

Ryan and I bought a home in Pacific Palisades.

Taking Trina with me, we created a powerful agency built around my original vision of promoting diversity. We covered the full spectrum of the modeling industry, crossing over into the glamor side of the business only when the right opportunity walked through the door.

I used my personal savings to fund the Hip-Hop Acting and Dance Studio with my daughter. The studio specialized in training actors and actresses for many of our commercial media clients.

Ryan opened Rhino's Training Academy where a staff of elite martial arts experts and professionally trained fighters would teach men, women, and children a free form of self-defense fighting techniques. Ryan's physical fitness training programs landed him major contracts with a number of governmental agencies.

He struck pay dirt by signing an exclusive long-term agreement with the Federal Bureau of Investigation for the Southern Region of the U.S. His programs worked complementary to the intensive physical training of the bureau.

After months of defensive maneuvering Monique Harding was convicted of being a participant in attempted kidnapping.

Due to her cooperation and testimony against the other defendants she received a 5-year sentence. The sentence was reduced to three years and two years' probation.

Paul Gregory's attorney Vernon Andretti withdrew his representation. Paul could no longer afford him. He ended up with Jabari Cooper's court appointed attorney.

He was convicted of all charges against him and received a sentence of 25-years to life with possibility of parole in 25 years. To this day he swears he did not know about the killings.

Roman Yee was convicted of aiding and abetting on two counts of murder, one count of kidnapping, one count of attempted kidnapping and a participant in a sex trafficking network. He received three consecutive 25-year terms.

Edward Alexander was promoted to Director of the Eastern Seaboard from Maine to Florida for Invisible Securities Corporation. He bought a home in New Jersey where he and Vanessa continued their relationship.

Vanessa's notoriety capitulated her already stellar career to another level. She worked out of the New York office and began a career in action movies. She and Edward married upon learning they were expecting an addition to their families.

Special Agent Samantha Jackson relocated to McLean, VA. She became the highest ranking African American woman within the Office of National Intelligence serving as the division chief of enterprise management. Her division advises Congress, senior leadership, The Office of Management and Budget and other external organizations on federal human capital laws.

Special Agent Nathan Gilbert retired from the FBI. He went to work for Invisible Securities Corporation as an international attaché. His main duties include working with principal law enforcements agencies and security forces in designated foreign countries. His specialty: prevention of human trafficking in the U.S. and abroad.

Richard Alexander relocated to Northern California and received a promotion as deputy director of Invisible Securities Corporation. His duties and responsibilities included overseeing all of the intelligence and security threats of ISC clients.

Chapter 70

November 22, 2018
Carter Lake, Iowa
3:00 p.m.

The End

Everyone was in attendance for the annual Alexander family Thanksgiving dinner. Vanessa and Ryan were included in our extended family.

After the blessing of the food, each person went around the circle sharing stories of why they were thankful this year.

My reflections were met with an outpouring of happy tears. I thanked my father for working secretly behind the scenes to help me take my company public. Learning of his ministrations from some initial investors had been a total surprise.

I ended my speech by sharing two valuable lessons that the ordeal of the last few months had taught me.

"First, never take the love of family for granted. It's more precious than gold. And two, manage my own financial affairs. All I can say is thank you and I love you all. I love you all."

 R. LaMont W. is a Personal Finance and Investment Educator. He is the financial consultant for the Greater Sacramento Literacy Group https://www.gsflg.org/. He is the author of "My 1st Investments Coloring Book", "A Beginners Guide to Wealth Building – Defined Contribution Plans" and the novel, "Never Judge a Book..."Originally from Berkeley, CA., he has a B.A. Degree in Psychology from the University of California, Davis and a Master's in Business Administration from Golden Gate University in Finance with an Investments Concentration. He is a former Investment Officer for the California State Teachers' Retirement System and resides in Sacramento, CA.
Website: www.ifiecorp.com
https://www.facebook.com/ifiecorp/